CORRUPTED BY A GANGSTA 2

Destiny Skai

Lock Down Publications and
Ca$h Presents

Corrupted by a Gangsta 2
A Novel by Destiny Skai

Destiny Skai

Lock Down Publications
P.O. Box 870494
Mesquite, Tx 75187

Visit our website
www.lockdownpublications.com

First Edition September 2018
Printed in the United States of America

Lock Down Publications
Like our page on Facebook: Lock Down Publications @
www.facebook.com/lockdownpublications.ldp
Cover design and layout by: **Dynasty Cover Me**
Book interior design by: **Shawn Walker**
Edited by: **Lauren Burton**

Stay Connected with Us!

Text **LOCKDOWN** to 22828 to stay up-to-date with new releases, sneak peaks, contests and more…

Submission Guideline

Submit the first three chapters of your completed manuscript to ldpsubmissions@gmail.com, subject line: Your book's title. The manuscript must be in a .doc file and sent as an attachment. Document should be in Times New Roman, double spaced and in size 12 font. Also, provide your synopsis and full contact information. If sending multiple submissions, they must each be in a separate email.

Have a story but no way to send it electronically? You can still submit to LDP/Ca$h Presents. Send in the first three chapters, written or typed, of your completed manuscript to:

LDP: Submissions Dept
Po Box 870494
Mesquite, Tx 75187

DO NOT send original manuscript. Must be a duplicate.

Provide your synopsis and a cover letter containing your full contact information.

Thanks for considering LDP and Ca$h Presents.

Acknowledgements

First and foremost I would like to thank all of my readers for their continuous support. Without you all, none of this would be possible. Thank you for allowing me to flood your minds with crazy plots and characters. I do this for y'all. If you haven't joined my reading group on Facebook please do so: Skai's Book Babies, to keep up with updates, new releases, contests and lots of laughs. Without further ado enjoy the story and leave a review when you're done. Your feedback is important to me. Thank you.

Destiny Skai

Chapter 1

Zuri

"Zuri," Brick called out, startling me. "Did you hear me?"

I glanced up at him, but I didn't say anything. My mind frame was too fucked up at that point.

"Baby. We need to talk," he repeated.

All I could do was sit and look into his eyes with a blank stare. The vivid picture of my brother embedded in my brain was killing me and my heart was so broken. It was cruel and inhumane to go live recording someone bleeding to death, instead of trying to help him. I swore I hated people. Legend and I didn't speak often and our bond wasn't the way it should've been. But, best believe when he stepped foot in Florida, he made sure we spent time together. My brother was the only one in the family that didn't cast me out or disown me. It wasn't that he agreed with me or our father's dealings, he understood what I faced growing up and my urges to feel loved. When I told him how my urges began, he felt guilty about his role in my advanced sexual activities. I could hear his voice, as the tears rolled down his brown cheeks. We looked so much alike.

"Zuri, I'm sorry. I had no idea that I contributed to this and I promise I won't turn my back on you. You're my sister and I love you so much." Legend hugged me tight and we cried in each other's arms.

"I don't want to talk right now. Will you just hold me?" The one person who loved me besides Daman and Brick was gone and I would never see him again. I was crushed.

"Yes."

I crawled into the bed and Brick climbed in behind me. The warmth of his body and his tender touch soothed me, but it would never heal me. The type of hurt I was feeling would never go away, and nothing would ever fill the hole in my heart. If I didn't have him during my time of need, I probably would've done something to hurt myself and my unborn child. My mind was boggled by the fact that a coward-ass nigga murdered him. All it could be was his status and money, because he didn't have beef as far I knew and from what he told me.

Legend was loaded with money because he ran all of South Florida, which included Dade, Broward and Palm Beach County from another state. Three years ago, he relocated to South Carolina and made return trips to conduct business. He left because he wanted to raise his son in the suburbs and guide him in a different path. And, to stay out of harm's way.

"I just don't understand why someone would kill my brother. He doesn't even live here. I will never get over this." And there I was, sobbing once again.

Brick squeezed me tighter. "I'm sorry, baby. I really am and I wish I could take all of your pain away."

"You can't. My heart will be broken forever."

I cried off and on for hours until I finally closed my eyes and drifted off to sleep.

***

Brick

For the first time in my life, I regretted pulling that trigger. Listening to Zuri scream and cry for hours fucked up my mental state badly. The pain I inflicted on her unintentionally was tearing me up on the inside and there was nothing I could do to make it better. No amount of money, bags or material items would heal her broken heart, and that came from her own mouth. However, my heart kept telling me I had to do something to take her mind off things. It would have to be really good, so I started thinking of different ways to put a smile on her face.

While she was sound asleep, I slipped from behind her and hit the shower. I made the water as hot as I could stand it and stood there in deep thought with both hands on the wall, staring at the floor.

"God, forgive me for cursing, but I fucked up and I fucked up big time. I guess this is what your message was for. If I would've followed my first mind and not gone there in the first place, he would still be alive, and my woman wouldn't be in there with a broken heart."

Moving my head from side to side, I chewed on my bottom lip as tears welled up in my eyes, before racing down my cheeks. Water splashed on the side of my face, mixed with my tears and trickled down my body. I cried for Zuri and myself. Me, because I knew what it felt like to have someone you loved gunned down and your eyes couldn't get that shit out the memory bank. The night my father was murdered, I was there but I didn't witness it, because I was in the house. No matter what the case was, it all hurt the same.

Unlike me, Zuri didn't have to see him up close and personal. She didn't have to smell the blood, or stare at him for hours on a cold, hard sidewalk, because they couldn't move the body before the investigation was complete. Zuri didn't have to witness her mother scream, kick and cry when the coroners took his body away or help wash the blood-stained sidewalk because the crime scene investigators were too sorry to clean it up. My mother's screams pierced my ears, as my past flashed in my mind.

"Nooo! Give him back. I just need more time with him." My mother held onto the gurney as they tried wheeling him away. *"Give me back my husband. Fernando, baby, wake up please. You can't leave me and Brandon on this earth alone."*

The healing process was a long road ahead, but I owed her a constant shoulder to lean on until her days and nights were easier to bear. Soon, I was able to get my emotions in check and shower. Before I went back into that room, my head needed to be on straight, so I could provide her with the proper care. Stepping from the shower, I dried my body off and draped the towel around my waist. My physique was in top-notch shape, but soon I would need to start back hitting the gym. Since I made it to the free world, I hadn't stepped foot into one.

Zuri was balled up on her side of the bed, clutching her body pillow tight when I walked into the room. She made a sound, so I rushed over to make sure my lady was okay, but her eyes were closed. I stood beside the bed and watched her sleep for a while longer and the groaning noise happened again. As I leaned down closer to her face, I realized she was crying in her sleep. The teardrops were plain as day. Being a witness to that shit didn't feel good at all.

I needed to touch her, so I dropped my towel and crawled into the bed with her. Zuri was easy to move, so I rolled her onto her back and tossed her body pillow to the floor. Gently I pushed her legs apart and positioned myself between them. Then I eased my body onto hers and planted soft kisses on her tear-stained face. Using my right hand, I rubbed the tip of my head against her lips until she was wet enough to penetrate. Pushing inside of her took my breath away. I sighed heavily.

"Ouu. Ssss."

Tonight, there wasn't going to be none of that freaky, wild shit I loved to engage in. Instead, I sided with making slow, sweet passionate love to her. My body moved with ease, as I grinded at a slow tempo inside my pussy.

Zuri's eyes fluttered and a soft moan escaped her soft lips. Both of her arms slid across my shoulders and made their way to the middle of my back. Caressing my body, she pulled me further down and buried her head in the crook of my neck. Sniffles followed soon after, confirming she was crying once again.

"I'll be here for you, baby. I promise I ain't going nowhere," I whispered softly in her ear. "But, I need you to remember that you pregnant."

Our skin created warm friction as our bodies collided, as I continued to stroke and slither against her body like a snake. Making love wasn't my forte, but I enjoyed the sensual connection that came along with it. Zuri's body tensed up, signaling an eruption was near. After ten minutes of constant grinding, my body followed suit and I laid down beside her and cuddled with my love. There were no words spoken, because nothing further needed to be said. The beating of our hearts together felt like good, old-fashioned acapella music from the early nineties and that was good enough for me.

The following day, I didn't feel any better about my actions and the guilt was winning. Zuri's painful cries made everything worse. Throughout the course of the night she would jump out of her sleep periodically in a cold sweat and a face full of tears. The crying seemed as if it was never ending. She cried so much until her eyes were swollen and damn near closed shut. I didn't want to leave her alone, but I had some loose ends to tie up.

"Stay in bed until I get back and if you need me call me. I won't be gone more than two hours. I promise."

She nodded her head.

Before I left I tucked her in and kissed her on the cheek. "I love you from the bottom of my heart."

Zuri nodded her head again, but she didn't say it back and she didn't need to because I knew how she felt about me.

***

On my way out the door, I observed a black Tahoe truck sitting across the street. The tints were fairly dark, but the dude inside was definitely white. It was probably neighborhood watch or some shit, so I kept it moving. Coop was standing beside his car engaged in what seemed like an intense conversation. He was so deep into it that he didn't notice me walk up.

"Man, why you trippin'? I mean, damn. I just left the goddamn house and you already calling about some bullshit." Coop was hollering like he was in the country.

That nigga's girl was always on ten when she couldn't see his ass in the flesh. At first, she was cool with it, but then she flipped on his ass when they moved in together. That was one thing that would aggravate me, but I knew for a fact me and Zuri wouldn't have those problems in the future. Or so I hoped. Coop turned around when I laughed and held the phone up so I could hear.

"Sit'cho ass in the house and watch some goddamn TV or better yet, do the damn laundry since you ain't do shit yesterday."

"Oh, I'm watching TV alright. I'm watching *Snapped,* nigga, so you better be careful," Danielle yelled.

"I ain't better do shit. We'll both be on muthafuckin' *Snapped*, so keep playing wit' me."

"Keep showing out in front of Brick. I know he listening, but he can't save you."

Coop laughed it off. "You trippin' for real."

Danielle had me cracking up, so I had to chime in. "Brick ain't heard shit."

"See, I knew it. You know he came home late last night?" Danielle thought she was slick trying to confirm his whereabouts, but I would always have my nigga back.

"Calm down, sis. We was together and I got in late too. We was chillin', so go easy on bruh." That was the truth.

"Chillin' my ass, that's a married man. He need to chill in this damn house and Brick, you need to be in the house with your woman. What the hell y'all hanging out late for?"

"My girl was cool wit' me coming in at that hour." It was the truth, but my issue was larger than coming in late.

"I need to talk to her, 'cause I ain't having that shit. Give me a day with her and you'll be on curfew."

"Nah, she straight. I gotta keep her away from you." There was no way in hell I was about to let Danielle taint Zuri's thought process.

Danielle continued to give him the business. "Coop, you better stop playing with me before I be a widow."

"Yo' ass wanted to be a housewife, so I made you one. Now go knit a nigga a sweater or some shit. Who the hell gon' pay the bills if we both laid up?"

"Don't get cute, nigga. I remember when I couldn't pull you out this ass."

"Shiiidd, pussy fie. How you think you got the ring in the first place?" Coop was steady cracking jokes.

"Ughhh," Danielle grunted into the phone. "Keep laughing. You ain't gone get what you want, but you will reap what you sew."

"Bae, I gotta go. I love you and I'll be home later."

"You better not be out late tonight and I'm not playing." Danielle hung up the phone and we both burst out in laughter. Coop scratched his head and opened the driver's door. "The shit a nigga go through."

We both got inside and I closed the door. "Danielle ass crazy. What the hell you did?"

"Shit, what I didn't do is the question." He backed out the driveway. "She was already mad 'cause I came home late, so she ain't wanna fuck, so I took it. Now, she pissed 'cause she wanted to fuck before I left and I said no. She was trying to be like me and take it, but I ran out the house."

That shit made me holler. "Bruh, you childish as fuck."

"You know Ion give a fuck. I wanted to make her ass mad. It ain't like a nigga cheating. Since we tied the knot six months ago, I haven't touched another female."

"That's good, bruh. I'm proud of you, but you know what she need?"

"What?" Coop's ears perked up when I said that.

"A baby."

That nigga smile turned upside down quick. "What the hell is that supposed to do?"

"She lonely. If she had somebody at the house wit' her, she wouldn't be on your trail. I'm tellin' you some good shit."

"Then I'll just buy her ass a puppy. We ain't ready for that yet."

"That ain't the same, bruh. Gon' blow the girl up. Shit, y'all married already and I don't see the problem. I done knocked Zuri up already. I ain't playin' no games."

Coop had one eye on the road and one on me with his head tilted. "Damn, you damn sholl ain't waste no time nuttin' in that."

"Aye it is what it is. I'm knockin' that down raw every chance I get."

"That's 'cause you fresh out and that nut super potent."

"Ion play games."

"Ole drippy-dick-ass nigga."

My mind went back to Zuri and my mood changed without warning. "Fuck all that. I got a problem on my hands."

His forehead became engulfed with wrinkles. "Who we gotta take out?"

"Nah, it's who we shouldn't have taken out."

"I'm confused." Coop missed the red light intentionally. "What's going on?"

"So last night after you dropped me off, I go in the house and Zuri sitting on the bed crying and shit. I'm asking her what's wrong, but she ain't saying shit. She was just sitting there, rocking with her phone in her hand. After like ten minutes, I get her to talk and she tells me that her brother was killed."

"What?" Coop was definitely confused.

"Legend was her brother."

"Get the fuck outta here."

"No bullshit, bruh. When I tell you I ain't get no sleep last night or this morning, I ain't get shit. She cried off and on all night." Peering out the window, I nodded my head. "I'm scared she gon' lose the baby if she can't keep it together."

"Damn." He sighed. "That's fucked up."

"Shit, who you telling? How you think I felt comforting her all night, knowing I'm the reason he dead?"

"I don' know what the fuck I would've did."

"I tried to tell her, but she didn't wanna talk." Coop slammed down on the brake, causing my body to jerk forward. "What the fuck you see?"

"I tried to make you bump yo' muthafuckin' head, 'cause you trippin'. Don't tell her what we did."

"Yeah, I thought about it after the fact. But bruh, you should've seen her, man. That shit broke a nigga heart."

"I feel that, but you tellin' her ain't gon' do shit but take us away from our loved ones and that ain't gon' bring her brother back." Coop reached over and tapped my shoulder. "And, y'all got a baby on the way. Telling her won't be good. Trust me."

"I know, bruh. This shit just fuckin' wit' me hard." I took a deep breath and rubbed my hand over my face. My ass was tired. "Take me by the corner store. I need a Red Bull."

"You need some liquor."

"Yeah, that too, but I need to get rid of this phone and Skeet shit. Take me by the crib first so I can get the new phones, and then we'll slide up on him at the corner he working."

"A'ight, cool. Then, after that," he paused and gave me eye contact before he continued. "The liquor store."

"That's cool."

He made some good points, but he didn't understand the battle I went through watching her grieve. That shit tore up every heart string in my chest. Keeping this a secret would always make me feel like she sleeping with the enemy. If things didn't get any better, I was gon' have to come clean and I would just leave Coop out of it. I wouldn't do anything to incriminate him, since I was the one that pulled the trigger. I was a man and I could take my sentence like a G. My only concern was Breanna and how that would affect her life going forward, 'cause the Lord knew I didn't want to leave her out here in the world without the guidance of her father. Just the thought of her being alone, made me realize she needed me more than Zuri would need closure in her brother's death.

Chapter 2

Daman

Throughout the first two years my prison sentence, I was never issued a detail. That shit wasn't for me and I could never imagine working for these muthafuckas, when I didn't ask to be here in the first place. But, since I started my operation, it was imperative that I was up close and personal with my shit when it came through. Two niggas tried stealing from me, so I made an example out of their asses and I haven't had any problems since then. It was also my escape from being in that cell all day.

My job was working in the laundry room and I loved that shit, because I didn't do shit pertaining to clothes while I was down there. I wasn't washing nan nigga boxers around this bitch. Many of they asses had shit stains from back-dooring other niggas when the lights went out, but that wasn't my business as long as they kept that gay shit out of my sight.

While my partners was working, I was kicked back listening to music, playing dominoes and shooting the shit. I was able to make a special arrangement and get my squad down here. There were only two that wasn't a part of it, but I was pretty persuasive when it came to making them join my alliance. It was either get down or lay down for good and get shipped home in a cardboard box. That was almost a year ago, so shit was sweet because I took care of all my hittas.

"Aye yo, Cee, make sure you don't wash my shit wit' nobody shitty draws. Put my shit in solo."

"Man, get the fuck outta here. How many times you gon' say that bullshit? Nigga, I heard you the first five times." Cee tossed my shit in the washer and slammed the door.

"Wash my shit wit' love, nigga."

"Bruh, you 'bouta wash yo' own shit." Cee laughed and sat in the chair next to me. "What's up wit' the phones?"

"They supposed to here today." I put my domino down on the table. "I'm about to lock the board up on y'all non-playing asses."

"I'm a pro at this shit." Tae put his domino down. "That's this nigga over here who can't play worth a damn."

Sam sat there staring at his dominoes before he went inside the spare pile. "Shit. Y'all niggas killin' me."

"Gon' wash them dishes, 'cause you about to lose anyway." This was my go-to game. I cleaned so many cats on the table at the yard gambling.

The sudden slam of the door caught everyone's attention. They immediately stopped talking and took a peek to see who was coming into my domain. "It's all good." Chuck gave me the confirmation I was looking for.

In walked Officer Tate, with her fine ass.

"This all y'all do around here?" She popped on the gum she was chewing loudly.

"Shiddd, what else we supposed to do in this muthafucka?" My eyes were locked in on her print. She loved to wear them tight-ass uniforms to entice the inmates with that fat ass. Just staring made my mouth salivate and my dick hard. Tate wasn't a bombshell, just the average-looking female with big lips.

Tate stood so close to me I could smell the mint on her breath. "Oh, I can think of a few things you could be doing." All that flirting was how we connected in the first place.

"Shit, so can I." I pushed the chair away from the table and stood up. "Finish that hand, Cee, and y'all know the routine." Before I walked off, I handed him my cellphone. "Be right back."

"Yeah."

Tate and I walked to the back of the laundry room and went into the bathroom. The light was already on so she walked in first and I closed the door. Spinning on her heels she turned to face me with her hands on my chest.

"I couldn't wait to get back to work and see you." My dick stiffened in my pants at her touch, as she caressed it and loosened my belt.

"You been thinkin' 'bout suckin' this dick?" I licked my lips seductively.

"You about to find out." Tate got down on her knees and freed the hammer. Then she looked up at me with a hunger in her eyes. "I see I ain't the only one anxious."

"That ain't no secret."

Tate licked around the tip in a circular motion slowly, while she jacked it. When it reached its full length, she eased it into her mouth inch by inch and went to work on it. Both of her hands were on my waist. Her head action was rapid and her hair weave bounced all over the place.

"Yeaahhh, bitch."

Whenever she gave me head, she liked to look in my eyes. That shit turned a nigga on. I held the back of her head, thrusting my hips forward aggressively. I could feel her backing up, but I gripped her shit tighter and jammed my dick to the back of her throat until she gagged.

Her grunt was muffled and spit dripped from the sides of her mouth, but I kept jabbing until she squeezed her eyes tight and they watered. I pulled my piece from her mouth.

"Mmm. Ssss." Tate licked the pre-cum from her lips.

"Stand up and turn around." Hesitation was never an issue whenever I told her to do something. She came out of them tight-ass uniform pants and bent over with her hands gripping the sink.

Longing to feel that pussy for the last few days, I glided that dick in with ease and gripped down on them hips. That shit was wet as fuck. Biting down on my lip, I drilled that ass hard from the back. Her cheeks bounced up and down. I smacked them hard.

Whap!

"Shit." She tossed her head to the side and closed her eyes. "Ahh. Ahh. S-shit."

Shit was getting real intense. While I beat her down, I slid my hand around her neck and gripped down on her throat. "Grrrr." That pussy had me growling like Tony the Tiger.

"I'm cummin'. I'm cummin'," she screeched and creamed all over my dick, making me slip out. I hawked spit between her cheeks and rubbed it over her booty hole. Then, I stuck my monster in that tight asshole.

"Nooooo," she screamed, springing forward. "That shit hurt."

I snatched her by the hair, snapping her head backwards. "If you want that rent paid, you gon' take this dick in any hole I put it in."

Tate straightened right up and arched her back so I could drop it back in. She could scream and holler all she wanted. I didn't give a fuck. The pussy was bomb as fuck, but I wanted to feel something a little tighter. In the middle of handling my business, the door opened. That didn't stop me, but I did look over my shoulder. It was Cee.

"Damn, bruh, I'll come back."

"Nigga, this live porn. You can watch." Tate was still moaning and I was still beating it.

"Rock on the phone." Cee had his head turned in the opposite direction.

"Hold up. I'm almost finished." It took another two minutes before I let off on the middle of her back. "Fuck." I was all out of breath and shit.

"Whoo!" I turned to face him with my dick still out. It wasn't no shame in my game and I was secure about my sexuality. "Gimme the phone."

Cee made sure his eyes were on my face and not my rod. "You gon' wash yo' hands?"

"Nigga, that's my phone."

"Yeah, but I use the muthafucka too."

"You don't know how many times I jacked my dick wit' the phone in my hand."

Cee handed me the phone. "You a nasty muthafucka."

"Ask ya mama about me."

"That ain't funny."

I put the phone to my ear. "What up, Rock?"

"Yo, what the fuck you was doing man?" His country accent was funny as shit.

"Getting some pussy. What's up?" I wiped the sweat from my forehead.

"I'm sitting across the street from her house and I just saw two gentlemen leave in a silver BMW," Rock stated.

That damning information had me pissed. My brow furrowed in frustration. "They both were in the house?"

The first thought to pop in my mind was maybe she just finished having a threesome or some shit. After all, she did try leaving me not too long ago. My better judgement knew it wasn't true, but the demon in me said to not put it past her.

"No. The guy in the BMW picked up the other one. They both look like drug dealers. They ain't at nobody's job early in the morning, while driving in a nice car, sporting high-priced clothes and jewelry."

"Why you say that, 'cause they black?" I chuckled into the phone. "Sounds like stereotyping to me. Don't tell me forty-five don' got to you too."

"Hell no. You know better than that shit. I have a lot of black friends."

"That's y'all favorite line. 'I have a lot of black friends,' " I repeated jokingly, imitating his voice.

"Daman, how long have you known me? Over twenty years. I'm a drug dealer, so I know what they look like." He tried justifying what he said.

Rock was actually a really good friend of mine. When I caught my bid, he was the only one from the free world to visit me regularly. I met him when he and his mom migrated into the neighborhood. The other dudes from the hood used to fuck with him because he was white, but not me. I actually gravitated towards him quickly. That muthafucka was huge. Rock was six foot seven and two hundred pounds solid, with reddish brown hair. These days, he was rocking a big-ass beard.

"Chill out, brotha. I'm just fuckin' witcha. You know I ain't got nothing but love for you."

"Same here, muthafucka. Now check yo' phone, because I sent you a picture of him." Rock laughed.

The multi-media message was on the screen, so I clicked it. The picture wasn't too clear, which deemed to be useless to me. "I can't see shit on that picture."

"Muthafucka, I ain't no damn photographer. Be happy with what I gave, 'cause that was the best I could do without being seen."

"A'ight cool."

"What you want me to do when I catch him alone? Kill him." Rock was ready to pop this nigga head open like a watermelon.

"Not yet. I need to find out who this nigga is first. Check around and see what you can come up with. Zuri is my only concern and I don't want her in any type of danger through retaliation."

"You know my work is always clean," Rock menacingly stated.

"Just stay back and I'll let you know when I'm ready for you to make a move." Tate tapped my arm, then looked down at her watch with her lips twisted up.

"I gotta go brotha, but holla at me later."

"Okay."

Pressing the end button, I looked outside the door. "Yo Cee get the phone."

He walked up with a dirty look on his face. "Gimme some tissue."

"What difference do it make? I still ain't wash my hands." I handed him the phone. "Get the shit so I can finish."

Cee took the phone from my hand and looked down at it. "Zuri calling."

"Send her to the voicemail." Then I closed the door in his face, so I could finish handling my business.

Chapter 3

Zuri

"You have been forwarded to the automated voicemail of 772-555-0199. Please leave your message after the tone."

"Ughh."

Aggravated, I tossed the phone on the bed and buried my face in my hands. That was the second time I called Daman to give him the bad news and he didn't answer. That shit was pissing me off because I knew he was sending me to the voicemail like I was five years old.

"He makes me so fucking sick with his black ass." A high-pitched scream boomed through my lungs, as I punched the pillow sitting beside me repeatedly. "I hate his ass."

At this point I knew I wasn't going to talk to him for a while, so I picked up the phone and sent him a text, since he didn't want to talk.

Daman: I know you sending me to the voicemail and that's fine, but I have something to tell you. Legend was killed, but I'm sure you know that already. My phone will be off for a few days, so you will not be able to reach me.

I was filled with so much anger and hate and I had no one to vent to. Brick left for a few hours, leaving me all alone and expecting me to be okay, but that wasn't going to happen. My fucking brother was dead and I'll never get to tell him that I loved him. My favorite pillow was beside me so I laid down and cuddled up with it.

"God," I shouted. "This is so unfair. Why did you let them kill my brother? I needed him." I rubbed my flat tummy. "I didn't even get the chance to tell him that I was pregnant."

All I could do was rock and cry, but I couldn't bring myself to close my eyes. Sleep was certainly far away in the future. Out of all days to log onto Facebook, I would do it at that time and get the shock of my life. There was no way in hell I was staying in the house. I had to get out and get some fresh air and make it back before Brick came home.

Jumping from the bed, I took off the shirt I slept in and put on an Adidas 'fit and sneakers. My hair was still plaited, so I didn't need to do anything except make the ponytail tighter. Then, I went in the bathroom to brush my teeth and wash my face. Once I finished up in the bathroom, I grabbed my keys, phone and purse and headed to the front door. The sun was shining, but there was a nice breeze so it wasn't so bad out. There was a truck sitting across the street I had never seen around my neighborhood before, but more than likely, they were checking out the vacant house that recently went up for sale. Hopefully, some nice and quiet people would move in because I hated noise. I started my car and backed out the driveway in a hurry.

***

The corner store was empty for the first time in history and that was very rare. Every hustler in the east was up there on a daily basis like they owned that shit. Guess the owner needed a break in front of his establishment. Shit, it wasn't like he wasn't a part of that shit anyway, he was probably supplying them with the drugs anyway.

A few minutes later, I was on 19th Street and tired of riding in silence, so I turned on the stereo. The music took control and my mind drifted, as I listened to "God's Plan" by Drake. While singing along, my thoughts drifted to Legend and it made me wonder why it was in God's plan to cut his life so short. He had a son that needed him and a woman that loved him without a shadow of a doubt. Sooner or later, I would have to call them, but now wasn't the time because I found it hard to speak on.

The further I drove, my chest grew tighter and tighter by the second. In less than one minute, I would be literally up the street from where Legend was killed. My mind was telling me to go to the crime scene, but my heart said it would be torture. I followed my heart and hooked a right on 441, towards Oakland. Fresh tears began to stream down my face like a waterfall and I was finding it hard to contain myself. However, I was too far from home and I was not about to call Brick to rescue me.

Daman still hadn't called me back, but I had a trick for his ass because I wasn't going to answer when he finally decided to hit me up. As a matter of fact, when Brick got back to the house, I was powering my phone off until I felt like being bothered.

My car ride came to an end and I finally reached my destination in the Devonhunt apartment complex. I parked my car and got out, leaving my items inside. The person I was looking for was sitting on the wall by her apartment. As I walked up, she had a distraught look on her face. But, I knew how she felt, because I didn't look put together, my eyes were red and my face was soaked in tears.

Kyra jumped down off the wall and stared at me with uncertainty, while studying the pain in my eyes. "Zuri, I'm so sorry to hear about your brother." Her voice was soft and filled with affection.

Just seeing her reminded me of all the times I cried on her shoulder when my heart was broken, or when it felt like the weight of the world was on my shoulders. That was the only person I could vent to when everything went wrong in my life. Kyra approached me with her arms out to embrace me and that's when I hauled off and popped her ass dead in the face. There was so much built-up anger from the things she said on Facebook about my past, and now, my brother's murder. She was gone wear an ass whooping for all the shit I was going through.

Blow after blow landed in her face. Fuck body shots, I wanted her to see this shit whenever her ugly ass looked in the mirror. My hand was wrapped around her hair, as I delivered so many uppercuts, I busted her nose. Kyra got ahold of my braids and yanked them, but I wasn't worried because her punches wasn't landing on shit.

"Ho'," she huffed. "You gone sneak me?" Kyra's big ass was out of breath.

"Fuck you, ho'. You know I don't fuck with you, period. I came over here to apply pressure, ho', 'cause you always got some slick shit to say on Facebook."

"Bitch, you should be home grieving." She kicked me on my thigh, but her words numbed me and I went berserk on that ass.

27

Some bionic strength came from somewhere and I slammed her on the ground and straddled her arms so she couldn't move. Grabbing her by the hair with both hands, I banged her head against the concrete. She was screaming her ass off. Then all of a sudden, I heard shouting before I felt a pair of hands grab me at the waist and pull me off of her. Whoever it was couldn't pull me far, because I wouldn't let go of her hair.

"Lil' mama, let her hair go," he said with a stern voice.

"No. Fuck her. She tried me."

"You done beat her ass, so let go." He tried to pry my hands away, but he was gone need an army to get me off her ass.

Right after that, another guy ran up and tried to pull her hair from my grip. "Zuri, let go."

The guy holding me shouted, "You know Floyd Mayweather daughter?"

My name falling from his mouth caught me off guard and that made me release the grip I had on Kyra's hair. "I don't know you. How do you know my name?" My stare was cold and I was waiting for anybody to try me.

Just by looking at him, I knew we didn't run in the same circles. He rocked a nappy fro and he was wearing a white tank-top with some cut-up jean shorts. "I knew your brother, Legend." His head hung low after he said his name, but his grip on Kyra remained tight as she tried to wiggle herself free. "That was my nigga. Sorry for your loss."

"Let me go." My eyes could no longer hold the water they contained and I broke down all over again. I just wanted to get the fuck away from there.

When I looked up at Kyra, she was just standing there watching me in silence. It looked as if she was crying too. My knees buckled beneath me and suddenly I felt faint. I could feel my body get weak, but the guy didn't let me fall. Instead, he escorted me to my car.

"You okay?" he asked sincerely, before opening up my door and placing me in the driver seat.

"I will be."

"Go home and take it easy, ma, you don' need to be 'round here fighting." He closed the door and walked off. "Sorry for your loss."

I sat there for a minute or so and I bawled hard with my head on the steering wheel.

***

Brick

"Pull up on the side." Coop parallel-parked against the sidewalk, then I rolled down the window. "Yo', come here."

"Hold on." Skeet threw up one finger, signaling me to wait on him to bust his lick. This nigga had on a Ferrari jacket in eighty-degree weather. He wanted to wear that bitch too bad. The sun was fading, but that didn't mean shit.

"That's a hustlin'-ass young nigga." My decision to recruit him was solely based on Coop's recommendation and so far, I was pleased with his performance.

"Yeah, I know. He been working for me since he was fourteen. Jit old girl out here trippin' and shit, so he gotta make sure his siblings eat and shit."

"Cold world, man." I shook my head in disbelief.

Skeet poked his head through the window. "What's up Boss?"

"Hop in." I instructed.

He quickly got into the back seat and closed the door. "What's going on? Everything kosher from last night?" His mouth was moving a thousand miles a minute.

"Yeah." Turning sideways, I eyed him. "Make sure you don't tell nobody shit. You don't know shit, you ain't seen shit, and don't comment on the subject, period. I can't afford no slip of the tongues."

"No doubt, boss. You can trust me."

"We working on that still, but I believe in you, though."

"Fa' sho," he replied.

Coop looked towards the back seat and chuckled. "Dawg, why the fuck you got on that hot ass-jacket? It ain't cold."

"Here you go, ready to crack and shit." Skeet leaned closer to the front seat.

"Damn right, 'cause we ain't got no insurance or Workers' Comp. You fall out and can't work, that's yo' bad. You gon' be up shit creek with no paddle."

"Boss," Skeet tapped my shoulder. "Where the fuck you get this nigga from? All the man do is crack jokes all day."

"This been my nigga since the sandbox days," I answered honestly. "He been a clown."

"You know I make yo' life better." Coop smirked.

"Fuck outta here."

"Oh, I forgot you don't like being sentimental in front of the employees." Coop was really killing himself laughing, but I ignored his ass. There was business that needed to be handled.

"Gimme your phone." I reached behind my seat and Skeet placed it in my hand. "You see that box on the seat back there?"

"Yeah."

"Open it and take that phone from outta there. That's your new phone, so anybody that you need or want to talk to, let them know you have a new number. This phone right here is dead."

"I need my contacts from out of there," he pleaded. "A lot of them numbers I don't know by heart."

The phone was on my lap, so I removed the back and took the battery out in search of the SIM card. When I found it, I handed it to him. "Here."

"Thanks."

"You seen Tone today?" Ever since Coop mentioned that he was getting high, I needed to protect my business.

"I saw that nigga earlier. He act like he was jiggin' or some shit," Skeet said with conviction.

Coop turned his head in my direction with a scowl on his face. "Bruh, I'm telling you, we need to get rid of this nigga. He bad for business. Shit, it ain't like he making us no money. You got yo' hardest worker right here."

"Yeah, I know, but I got this. Trust me."

"Keep on and I'm gon' rock the nigga," Coop assured me with a harsh and convincing tone.

"Just chill. He begged for a last chance, so if he short when we check in, it's a wrap."

Skeet tapped the seat. "We done? My block 'bouta start booming and I gotta meet up with this nigga that want a half a brick."

"Yeah, we good. I'll holla at you later." Skeet got out the car and stopped by the window. "Be safe out here," I told him.

Skeet lifted his shirt. "I stay strapped."

Rolling up my window, I sat back in the seat and closed my eyes for a minute or so. "Shit." I jumped up quickly, reaching for my phone. It slipped my mind that I was supposed to be checking on Zuri to make sure she was okay.

"What happened?" Coop asked with great concern.

"I was supposed to check on Zuri."

"Yeah, you better call her now." By the time he said that, I had already dialed her number.

Patiently waiting on her to pick up, I didn't get anything but her voicemail. So, I tried again. Same thing.

"Do you need to go and check on her?" he asked.

"Nah. She probably sleep." I put the phone in the cup holder. Then I rested my head on my hand. "Just go to the warehouse so we can get rid of this damn car."

"Yeah," he replied before turning up the radio.

I leaned my head against the headrest and closed my eyes and thought about Zuri. To say I wasn't worried would be a lie, because I wasn't sure what she was capable of. As far as I knew, she could've been suicidal. We had only been together for a short amount of time, so I was still learning her behavior. Granted that I was good at studying people. Truthfully, I believed she was okay and I was panicking for no reason.

The bright light shined in the car, getting my attention. When I looked up, we were pulling up at the warehouse. The sun had disappeared, allowing the moon and stars to take over the sky. Coop drove us to the very last aisle in the cut and stopped in front of our bay.

"Pop the trunk." Quickly going to the back, I lifted the trunk and grabbed my duffle bag, then put on a pair of black leather gloves.

Taking my keys from my pocket, I removed the padlock and slid the door open. The car was an older model Nissan Altima and since it was mainly a female car, it was what we preferred to work out of. In a few days, we would have to get a new one. I removed the old tag and replaced it with a new one, got inside and turned on the engine.

We drove out to the Lockhart Stadium on Commercial Boulevard. The lot was big and empty enough for me to accomplish what I set out to do. It was dark and the only thing that could be seen were cars in passing. Coop followed me to the back of the lot and turned off the high beams. Hopping out the car, I wiped down the steering wheel and door handles with some vinegar. The smell of the gas was loud and filled the car. I picked up the can and doused it with gasoline. With my belongings in hand, I lit a match and tossed it on the vehicle. The flames spread quickly like a wildfire and we got the hell out of Dodge. By the time we made it to the stop sign, we heard the explosion.

Chapter 4

Zuri

One week later

As I sat on the edge of Brick's bed, a heavy flow of tears cascaded down my face and dripped onto my chest. In my arms I held a picture frame close to my heart that housed a photo of me and Legend when we were younger. Never in a million years did I think I would be saying goodbye to my only brother forever. He was just about to celebrate his thirtieth birthday that weekend. The cold-hearted bastard that pulled that trigger had no idea of the pain they put me through.

A few days ago, Brick called my job to inform them of the tragedy. I had no idea what he said to them, but they granted me two weeks of bereavement. That was a blessing in my eyes, because there was no way I would be able to focus on work.

Friday rolled around quicker than I expected and I dreaded every second of it. My heart felt as if it were about to explode at any minute. The pain of just imagining how he died in agony was so unbearable. That was something I would never wish on my worst enemy. Not even Kyra's funky ass.

The viewing was scheduled to start in less than two hours and I was not ready to come face-to-face with his lifeless body resting in a casket. Honest to God, I would give my left lung to have him back again. To hear him say, *"What it do, baby sis?"* would mean the world to me.

"Baby, you okay?" The sound of Brick's voice made me stop rocking and open my eyes.

"Not really." He walked up to me and took the frame from hands, placing it gently on the dresser.

Brick stood over my limp body and took me into his arms. The energy I needed just wasn't there. "We're going to get through this together. I promise." He was so remorseful. "I hate seeing you suffer like this."

The thing I loved about Brick was his sensitivity towards me and my feelings. No matter how hard he was in the streets, he managed to leave it on the porch before encountering me. Firmly, I grabbed him at the waist and squeezed him tight, trying to keep it together.

"I can't help it. Every time I think about him, I cry. It's too hard to keep myself together."

Brick kissed the top of my head before stroking it. "It's okay to cry. You need to grieve. I'm just worried about the baby. All the stress isn't good for your pregnancy."

He was absolutely right, but he should try telling that to my heart. My crying was the least of his worries. If he even caught a whiff of the fight between me and Kyra, he would explode and I would never hear the end of that.

"I'm trying." I sniffled.

"That's all that matters," he said sweetly. "Once I get my business in order, you and I are going away for a few days. I believe that would do you some good."

Nodding my head up and down, I wiped my eyes. "Okay."

"Get up so you can take a bath and get dressed so we can go. I ran your bath water already." Brick pulled me from the bed and escorted me to the bathroom.

The tub was filled with bubbles, but I was merely expecting just a tub full of water. I removed his oversized t-shirt I'd slept in and stepped in slowly. The temperature was almost like a sauna, but I needed it. My body sunk until the water level was at my neck.

"I'm going to give you five minutes to soak and I'll be right back."

"Okay." The second he walked away, I closed my eyes and relaxed.

There was so much going on in my mind and I didn't know how to deal with it all. According to my trapped calls, Daman had been trying to reach me, but I blocked his number. I was still mad at him and I wasn't ready to talk to him. It was probably wrong, but I didn't care. If that's what I needed to do to get away from him, then so be it. I was certain one of Legend's henchmen spoke with him and gave him the update. Especially since they were all doing business together. It was funny how Legend and Daman's relationship never dwindled after our secret surfaced. The only bond that was severed was our relationship with Mehzani and that was by force. Hopefully, I would get to see her at the viewing. Ever since Cruella de Vil split us up, we never saw each other again. She went as far as moving away to keep me from coming around. The last words she ever said to me when I showed up on her porch cut me deep and the look in Mehzani's eyes were filled with pain. She was still a little girl and barely understood what was going on.

Mehzani was sitting on the porch eating ice cream when I walked up. "Hey, Zani." I smiled. It had been a month since I last saw her.

"Zuri!" she screeched, jumping up from her seat and running towards me. "Are you coming back to live here?"

She jumped into my arms and I held her tight. "No, sweets. I'm never coming back, but I will come back for you."

"When?" she asked, as I placed her back on her feet. "I miss you." Mehzani dropped her head. "I'm sorry for calling the police. We'd still be together if I didn't say anything."

Her innocence was so pure and it hurt me to think that she blamed herself for our separation. Kneeling down to make sure we were eye to eye, I tried explaining the best way I could. "What happened that day is not your fault. Daddy and I did some things that we shouldn't have and I'll explain it to you when you get older."

"Auntie said you were being slutty with Daddy and you belong in a mental hospital. She said he abused you."

Shit was already bad and this ho' was fucking with my sister's mind-frame with the dumb shit. I swear, I hated her ass with a passion. "Auntie is stupid, so don't listen to her. Daddy didn't abuse me. He loves me. But, the love we shared with one another is frowned upon, but don't worry about all of that."

"Oh, well does that mean he didn't love me?" Her eyes seemed saddened, yet confused.

"Of course Daddy loves you."

"Get the fuck from around here, you nasty-ass whore. I don't need you corrupting her." Cruella de Vil was standing on the porch with her hands on her hips. *"Mehzani, didn't I tell you not to talk to her? Get in the house."*

"But, she's my sister." Mehzani pouted with her arms folded.

"Fuck you, Debra, you always talking shit. You bird-brain raggedy ho'. Come down these steps and I'll beat your ass."

"That's why I never liked your ass. You disrespectful and think you know it all, but I'll lay you out, niece or not."

"Do it, bitch, I'm waiting." I pushed Mehzani to the side, as she walked in my direction. When she was within arm's reach, I reached out and touched her ass.

Debra knew she couldn't whoop me and I showed her I was nothing to play with. The next door neighbor and his son broke up the fight and she took Mehzani in the house, and that was the last time I saw my sister.

"I'm back." I opened my eyes to find Brick sitting on the side of the tub. Those were the fastest five minutes in history. He cleaned my face with the rag he held in his hand. "Damn, baby. I wish shit would've played out differently. You breaking my heart right now."

"What do you mean?" He had me a little confused.

Brick paused and just looked at me. For some reason, it looked as if he wanted to cry with me. He took a deep breath and stroked my cheek. "I just wish this never happened to you."

"Me too."

Brick lathered up the washcloth and bathed my upper body, as I sat there helpless, crying. "You are a godsend and I don't know what I did to deserve you. Who knows where I would be right now if it wasn't for you."

He stood up, then lifted me from the water, raised me to my feet and washed the rest of my body. "I'm not that much of one. I've caused you more heartache than you realize."

"What do you mean?"

"Nothing. Come on so we can go." Brick wrapped me in a towel and carried me to the bedroom.

***

It was a few minutes before five o'clock in the evening and we were the first ones at the church. And, that's exactly the way I wanted it to be. The first hour was for the family and after that, the place would be swarming with fake niggas and bitches showing fake love. Due to his popularity, I knew his viewing was going to be a circus, so I wanted to get in there and spend my final time with him in peace without folks passing out fake-ass hugs for comfort. For all I knew, his killer was going to be amongst the crowd, rocking his RIP shirt. That was also the reason his viewing was held at Mt. Olive Baptist Church, instead of the funeral home. It was huge and there was plenty of space.

Brick opened up the passenger door. "Come on." He grabbed my hand, closed the door and escorted me to the front of the church. "You ready?"

Frantically, I shook my head. "No."

"Come on, let's do this. I'm right here with you." Brick placed his hand on my waist and ushered me to the inside.

"Good evening." We were greeted by an usher.

"Good evening," Brick replied, being that I was too distraught to open my mouth.

The sound of the soft music was heartbreaking and clarification that one had reached the pearly gates to be with the Lord. I signed my name on the first line in the guest book and took a deep breath to prepare myself for the finale. As we walked down the aisle, my chest grew tighter and tighter with every step and water began to pour from my eyes like a faucet. I could see his body plain as day in his clear casket with gold angels on all four corners, which was surrounded by tons of flowers. Mine stood out the most. It was a teal and white arrangement on top of the casket, with a picture of Legend, Mehzani and I when we were younger, planted in the middle. It was a special piece. Each flower was dyed because teal was Legend's favorite color and I owed it all to Brick, since he paid for it. His fiancée, Shakira, reached out to me and asked if I wanted to assist her in planning my brother's burial, so of course I obliged.

Legend looked so peaceful, yet dapper in his all-black Gucci jogging suit. Shakira wanted him to be dressed this way for the viewing. Then, he would be buried in a Gucci suit on Saturday. She sent me pictures of the suit and I had to admit it was nice, but I swear she was too obsessed with the Migos, because she dressed him like Quavo. His dreads were neatly groomed, resting on both shoulders, and his shape-up was sharper than Steve Harvey's. Just seeing him lying there was unbelievable. No matter how much I tried to force myself to see it was all a dream, I had to come to the realization that his death was real and he was never coming back.

"Legend!" I screamed and held onto the casket with both arms. My face was above his, but I couldn't touch him. The glass had us separated. "Come back, pleeease."

Brick tried to pull me away, but I was too strong. All of my dead weight lay against the coffin. "Zuri, stop."

"Noo," I screamed louder. "This my brother. Let me go. I want my brother back." He wouldn't let me go, so I started bucking and sobbing. "God, please give him back."

"Sir, let me help you." I heard a voice say, but I didn't see a face.

"Legend's not gone. This is a dream. Wake me up. Wake me up. Wake me! Shake me!" I screamed belligerently.

"Zuri, let go." Brick was still trying to pull me away. Then I felt a pair of hands prying my fingers off the casket.

"Give him back. I just want my brother back. Take my baby instead. Kill whoever shot him instead."

After fighting for what felt like forever, they were able to get me away from the casket and onto the pew. "Zuri, baby, I need for you to try and stay calm please, 'cause you don't mean what you're saying."

Brick held me close to his chest and I could feel the rapid beat of his heart. "Here." He handed me some tissues to clean my face.

This was just as hard as I imagined. I was not prepared to let him go whatsoever. A little while later, I could hear a group of people come in, so I sat up to see who was coming in. To my surprise, it was Daman's evil-ass sister, Debra. We immediately locked eyes.

"This is supposed to be a time for family only. What the hell is *she* doing here?" Debra was ghetto trash at its finest.

Today was not the day and I knew my mouth, so I refrained from cussing her ass out in the house of the Lord. Brick turned to see where the commotion was coming from.

"Who the hell is that?" he asked.

"My dad's old, ghetto-ass sister. She always talking shit. If she come over here with the bullshit, I'm beating her ass on sight."

"She ain't gon' do shit and neither are you. Did you forget you pregnant? I'll handle who and whatever come your way."

Debra stopped in front of the casket and glanced at Legend with those fake-ass crocodile tears. My brother didn't fuck with her either, so I don't know why she was doing the most. Shakira was amongst the crowd coming in and I could see LJ standing at her side. He was the spitting image of my brother and it was crazy. It was like he carried that boy himself.

After Cruella de Vil dabbed her eyes with a napkin, she casually walked in my direction. I was about to stand up, but Brick grabbed my arm and pulled me back down.

"Don't move." I did like he said, but I was ready to pop off on that ass and drag her all through the church.

Debra kept some distance between us, as she stood there with her hands on her hips. "This time is for family only. Visitation to the public is at six o'clock."

"Fuck you and I am family. My brother didn't fuck with you, so why you here?" My irritation showed because I started biting my bottom lip.

"I'm his auntie, that's why." She rolled her eyes. "I cast you away a long time ago."

Brick spoke up. "Listen, get the fuck from over here and find you a seat and sit' cho ass in it. My girl grieving and I'm not in the mood for none of this fuck shit."

"Oh, so you brought you a thug in here for protection." She fanned herself with the church fan she was holding. "Oh, that's funny."

"You know damn well I don't need protection from you. I done beat your ass already. You better act like you know that I'll dig up in that ass and not how you want me to." Her ass was two seconds from getting slapped and I meant that shit.

"Girl, please. You ain't beat my ass and you heard what I said. So, if you don't want these problems, I suggest you and thug life roll up outta here."

Debra rocked on her heels with her arms folded like she was waiting for us to get up. "Did you tell him that you was a whore at a young age and used to fuck your daddy? Did you—"

That was the last thing she said before my fist met her teeth, causing her to stumble backwards. I was all over her ass and there wasn't shit she could do about it, but kick and scream like the bitch she was. Brick tried pulling me away, but she had my braids wrapped around her hand.

"Let my hair go, you evil bitch," I shouted in a rage.

Brick grabbed Debra's hand. "Let her hair go." When she wouldn't release my hair, he twisted her wrist until she let go. "You okay?" he asked, pulling me away from her.

I raked my braids out of my face. "I'm good."

"You bitch, you just wait." Debra wiped her bloody lip.

Two of my cousins rushed to Debra's aid and I could hear one of them ask if she was okay. Derrick looked in our direction with a mean mug. "What the fuck wrong with you, Zuri, putting yo' hands on my old girl?"

"Fuck her. She shouldn't have ran up on me talking that shit." I looked his ass up and down, because he knew I wasn't backing down. Derrick and I had fought before, so his ass was well aware I didn't play. When I first moved in with them, he'd tried to show off in front of his company like he ran shit, so I maced him and beat his ass with his mammy's bat.

Derrick tried to ease up on me quick, but Brick stepped in front of me, blocking his path. "Nigga, run up on my girl like you crazy and I'll knock yo' fuck ass out in here."

He stood there and looked Brick up and down. "Move, nigga."

"Nah, fuck boy, hit me since you so tough," Brick spat. If he knew like I did, he would sit his ass down, but he didn't have to 'cause the staff was running over in our direction.

"Break this up or we gone have to ask y'all to leave." It was the same man who helped Brick get me calm earlier.

"I called the police already," Debra shouted with her ignorant ass.

"We leaving." Brick grabbed my arm. "Let's go, 'cause I'll body this muthafucka right in this church."

"Yeah, leave, because she ain't wanted here." Debra kept talking shit, but it was gone be a matter of time before I ran into her ass again.

"Fuck you, bitch. You'll see me soon." I was pissed.

On our way out, Brick was literally pulling me out the church by my arm at a fast pace. I spotted a female in the back wearing dark shades. She looked like Mehzani, but I couldn't get a good look at her face because we were moving too fast.

"Wait!"

"No. We have to go. Especially if that bitch called the police." Brick kept walking.

"I think I saw my sister. Just go wait in the car and if you see the police, then leave, but I need to see if it's her. Please. I haven't seen her in years."

Brick stopped and looked at me. "I'm not leaving you and I'm not letting you go back in there by yourself, so come on. We'll check together."

Both of us walked back inside to where I saw her, but she was gone just that fast. I was a little torn on the inside, but I knew I would see her tomorrow. At least, I hoped so anyway.

Destiny Skai

Chapter 5

Mehzani

Seeing Zuri for the first time in years put a painful strain on my heart and brought back old memories. The last time I saw her face, she promised to come back for me and she never did. Deep down, I felt some resentment towards her and the same time, I wanted to build a bond with my sister. My first thought was to run up and hug her, but instead, I did the opposite and ran away. Upon entering the church, I heard the commotion, but I wasn't for sure who it involved until I heard her voice. Time passed us by tremendously, but I could never forget what she sounded like when she was angry.

To be reunited with Zuri had been something I prayed on for years, but my actions caused us to split up in the first place. If I would've kept my mouth shut, none of this shit would have happened. I divided the family. It was my fault we were no longer close-knit and Daman was in prison. For years, I've regretted opening up my big-ass mouth. I should've left well enough alone and kept people out of the family business. It was too late to go backwards now. All I could do was move forward with my life and pray that Zuri and I got a second chance because it was too late for Legend.

When I found out he was killed, it broke my heart that we were never reunited. Debra was to blame for that. From the time she sent Zuri away, she made sure I was sheltered away from my siblings. We had no contact whatsoever. Even when Daman tried to reach out to me, I wasn't allowed to talk to him. Every letter he sent, Debra trashed it. My aunt was a really fucked-up person and I came to realize that when I was high school, which was why I couldn't wait to go off to college. My freshman year consisted of heavy partying and lots of sex with this fine-ass football player named Rashad.

One night, he had a wild ass party at his apartment. At first, I was reluctant about going but I changed my mind, since we had been kicking it for a month and I wanted to get out and have some fun. When I got there, I was a little hesitant about drinking for the first time, but Rashad assured me I would be okay and that he wouldn't let anything happen to me. Needless to say, I believed him and had my first drink. It had me feeling so good, I continued to scoff down cups of liquor like I was a professional. After my fifth or sixth cup, I was out of there. Rashad even had me smoking weed. I was fucked up to the point that he had to carry me to his room. He put me in the bed and started kissing all over my neck, but all I wanted to do was sleep that shit off.

"Rashad, please. I just want to sleep." I tried pushing him off of me, but his five-eleven, buck-ninety frame was too heavy.

"Come on, Mehzani." He had his hand on my breasts, caressing them.

"I don't feel good," I pleaded.

"I know and I'm trying to help you with that. I'll make you feel good, I promise." He was trying to convince me to take that next step by taking my hand and placing it on his erection. It was thick and hard as hell.

I eased my hand back. "I just need some sleep, please."

"Okay. Okay, I'll stop."

Rashad accepted my response, adjusted his dick in his pants and left the room to go back to the party. Sometime after that, I went to sleep. When I woke up he was between my legs, eating me out. I was still fucked up, but it felt good so I went with the flow, grinding against his face.

"Mmm," I moaned.

He looked up at me with those chestnut brown eyes and licked his lips. "I told you I could make you feel good."

He was right about that, 'cause I was on cloud nine. We ended up having sex a few times that night and the next day. That was the beginning of our sexual encounters and heavy partying. At first, it was just liquor and weed, then we started popping pills and being careless. That was when I ended up pregnant. I wasn't ready to be a mother and I certainly couldn't tell my aunt. Hell, I was still learning life, so I knew I couldn't raise a child. Rashad agreed with me because he wasn't ready either, so we made a conscious decision to terminate the pregnancy. During my visit to the doctor, I also learned that he gave me chlamydia. I was livid because he was the only person I was sleeping with and I never contracted an STD. He apologized for cheating and like a stupid naïve girl, I stayed with him.

One would've thought I learned my lesson, but I didn't and allowed him to steer me in the wrong direction. Messing with Rashad really fucked me up mentally. I was missing classes due to the late-night parties and turning up, but I was so hooked I couldn't stop. All we did was smoke and fuck every day, even when my period was on sometimes. We would just do it in the shower. Shit didn't get bad until I started failing classes and had to pay out of pocket. Doing that put my ass in a hole and I couldn't make the payments, because I didn't have a job. Rashad would help out sometimes, since he had a scholarship for a full ride for football. When I called home to tell Debra, she advised me that I needed to come back home, since I wasn't doing what I needed to do. I ended up leaving the school and going back home and lost all contact with Rashad immediately.

Quickly, I found myself mixed up with old friends that partied on a daily basis. During one of my smoke sessions with my homeboy, he laced the blunt with some flakka and the rest was history. That shit fucked me up in the worst way, but thanks to my addiction I met a man that really cared for me and my wellbeing, so it was safe to say things really did happen for a reason. If I wasn't hooked on drugs, I would've never met Gucci. He was my world and I loved him with every breath in my body.

After my stroll from memory lane was over, I glanced around the church and Legend's funeral was jam-packed with the neighborhood drug dealers and thots. Some of them looked as if they had just left the club and drove straight to the church. I noticed Zuri and her dude were seated on the front row with Shakira. I wanted to go and sit with the family, but it just didn't feel right. I was the black sheep and it was uncomfortable, not knowing how they would feel about my presence. My phone vibrated on my lap and I immediately figured it was Gucci, since I didn't tell him where I was going. He didn't even know my brother was murdered. That was the part of me I wanted to deal with on my own. Gucci did more for me than any man I'd been in a relationship with, and my personal family affairs was something I didn't want him to witness. It was too harsh and frowned upon and I didn't want to be judged by him. Finally looking at the phone, I read the text message.

Debra: Bring me an obituary, 'cause these bitches won't let in
Mehzani: Who?
Debra: Security in the front said I can't come in 'cause of what happened yesterday with your sister
Mehzani: Okay

After my last text to her, I put my phone away. I couldn't lie, that shit was funny as hell, but that was her problem though. Ain't nobody tell her to come in here acting like a damn fool, but no matter where she went, Debra always acted as if she had no common sense or home training.

The pastor was preaching about dying young and being saved. I felt the sermon was a message for me and I should take heed to it. Even though I kicked my drug habit, I still had a long way to go and Gucci was there every step of the way. I couldn't have prayed for a better man. Not even the Ciara and Russell Wilson prayer would've worked for me.

After bringing his message to a close, the preacher made his announcement. "It is now time for reflections, please be courteous and limit your time to two minutes, please and thank you."

The pastor walked away and took a seat in his chair. The first person to walk up was our uncle Jimmy. He was wearing a bright orange suit and a pair of patent leather white shoes. He had the wettest gray and black Jheri curl, like he stepped fresh off the commercial set for Soul Glow. He grabbed the microphone, tapped it a few times, then cleared his throat like he was about to do a solo.

"Let the church say Amen."

"Amen," the church responded.

"Ooh, it's a wonderful day today. I'm happy to see that my nephew touched so many people, and I see a few faces I haven't seen in a while. I just want to say thank you for coming and I'm sad it had to be this way. For all of you who don't know me, I'm Uncle Jimmy."

On everything I love, I was trying my best to hold in my laughter, but it was hard to do. If I wasn't trying to stay hidden, I would've recorded his ass with my phone to laugh at later. The man was a flat-out comedian. I could remember him coming over to our house growing up. He was my dad's oldest brother, so he would check on us all the time to make sure we were okay.

"I used to keep Legend when he was a little boy. That rascal knew he was horrible. I remember one time, I told him if he ever had to pee in public and he couldn't make it to the bathroom, just pull out his winky and go. So one day we were in the grocery store and I was talking to this young lady. Nephew pulled my pants leg and said, 'Jim-Jim I have to pee.' I ignored him and told him to wait a minute, so I can get her phone number. The next thing I knew, the lady screamed and when I looked down, nephew was pissing on her foot." The entire church burst out into laughter, including Jimmy.

"Let's just say that I didn't get her phone number. Anyway, before I step down, I want to sing a song for my nephew."

The pastor looked at Uncle Jimmy and held up two fingers but he ignored him, cleared his throat once more and carried on, like he was in a room by himself. "The train is coming and you don't need no ticket to climb aboard."

Jimmy was definitely feeling his song. He was swinging his arms back and forth while he continued to sing. "The train is coming and you don't need no ticket to climb aboard." He stopped singing, but he continued to swing his arms.

"Woo," he said as he patted the casket. "I'm gone miss this boy."

By the look on the pastor's face, you could see he was ready for him to go and take his seat. Jimmy was well over his two minutes. Instead of the pastor saying anything, he stood up, hoping he would get the hint. But, when he didn't, Jimmy's wife got up and escorted him off of the stage. I was laughing so hard until my stomach started to hurt. The lady with the Easter basket on her head sitting beside me looked over at me, but she quickly turned her head when I mean-mugged her ass.

"What the fuck you looking at? That's my uncle and I can laugh whenever I feel like it, while you staring in a bitch face."

Once Jimmy was finally out of the way, a few more people came up and spoke about Legend.

After the last person stepped down, the preacher asked if there was anyone else that would like to say anything. The church was so quiet you could hear a pin drop. Then suddenly out of the blue, I heard hollering and screaming. The sound of Zuri's cries ripped through my chest. My own tears started to stream down my face and I couldn't take it anymore. We both lost someone we loved and she needed to know I was still here. Grabbing my purse, I stood up and made my way down the aisle. Two of the ushers were surrounding her when I walked up. Her man glanced at me and turned his attention back to her, but he had to do a double-take. Then, he looked at me funny. Instantly, I recognized him as Gucci's cousin, Brick. He didn't say anything, just simply turned his attention back to my grieving sister.

"Excuse me." I tapped one of the ushers on his shoulders. "This is my sister and I would like to comfort her." He backed up, then I kneeled down in front of Zuri and placed my hands on top of hers.

Zuri's head rose slowly and the moment we made contact, her eyes stretched wide when she saw my face. "Mehzani?" she said in a questionable tone.

"It's me, sis." To my surprise, she sat up in her seat and hugged me tight. I did the same.

"Mehzani, I missed you so much," her voice cracked, as she continued to sob.

"I missed you too."

"They killed our brother, Zani."

"All we have is each other," I replied.

We embraced one another for what seemed like an eternity. The usher placed his hand on my shoulder. "They're about to do the last glance. Can I have you to sit beside your sister, please?"

My arms wouldn't release her and all I wanted was to hug her a little longer, but I knew it wasn't the time or place for a reunion. Slowly, I rose to my feet and sat down in the empty spot beside her. While we watched everyone say their goodbyes to the one and only Legend in Broward County, we held hands as if we would be separated once more. Through my peripheral vision, Brick could be seen holding her other hand. My first impression when he was sitting in the car with Gucci was that he wasn't a very sociable person, and it was funny that he was Zuri's man all along and the link to finding her. That made me wonder if we would've crossed paths under different circumstances, like one of the cousin's family gatherings.

After the last set of people walked past us, the funeral home workers pushed the casket close to us, so we didn't have to get up. And, Lord, why did they do that? Shakira started screaming and grabbing ahold of the coffin, causing LJ to do the same.

"Why did you leave me? You promised you would never leave," Shakira screamed and hollered at the top of her lungs, as she held on to our nephew.

The remainder of my heart shattered into a million more pieces, seeing her react that way. Seconds later, Zuri was right behind her. Brick held on to Zuri to keep her from getting up. He was silent as he restrained her as much as possible. It was hard to keep her in place because she was bucking uncontrollably.

"They killed my brother," Zuri shouted. "Give him back, please. God, give him back."

I tried to help Brick hold Zuri, but that damn girl was still strong as hell. Finally, the ushers pushed his body away and ended the service. It was too much to bear and shit wasn't about to get any better, as long as he was still in her sight.

On the way out the doors of the church, Brick held onto her for dear life, as I walked behind them. Based on my observation, I had come to the conclusion that my siblings remained close over the years and that made me feel some type of way. While the two of them remained close, I was forced to face the world alone. The idea made me a little sad, but due to the circumstances, I couldn't really blame them.

Brick looked over his shoulder at me. "Follow me." I nodded my head and strolled behind the couple slowly. We stopped alongside a Mercedes Benz coupe. He popped the locks and put Zuri in the front seat. I waited patiently to see what he wanted. After he closed the door, he faced me and leaned against the car.

"Do you remember me?" he asked.

"Yeah." My arms were now folded against my chest. "You're my boyfriend's cousin."

Brick nodded his head. "I am." Shoving his hands into his pocket. "So, y'all real sisters?"

"Yeah. Same mama and daddy."

"That's what's up." The bewildered look on his face told me he had more questions for me. "Why I never saw you before? Y'all not close?"

At first I hesitated, but there was no point in keeping it a secret, because I'm sure he would question Zuri about it later. "No. We were separated when we were younger and this is our first time seeing each other in years."

"Damn, that's crazy." Brick looked in the direction of the cars and stood upright. "The cars are moving. You going to the cemetery?"

"No."

"Come here. I have something for you." Brick popped the trunk and walked away.

Of course, I was curious as to what he had for me, so I walked over without hesitation. He was rambling through a bag when I walked up and a few seconds later, he pulled out a cellphone. It looked like a burner.

"Take this phone and keep it on you at all times. When she's out of her slump, I will have her to call you. Zuri is in a fucked-up place and she's going to need you eventually. I can only do so much and since she lost a sibling, it will be important to work on y'all relationship."

I took the phone from his hand, examining it closely. It was a burner alright. "I'm looking forward to it."

"Okay. I'll be in touch."

"Alright." I stood there, clutching the phone tightly in my hand. The day I had been waiting on had finally presented itself and I couldn't wait to sit and have a heart-to-heart with my sister. All I had to do was hold the phone until it rang. So, let the waiting game begin.

Chapter 6

Brick

My feet dragged slowly through the evenly cut grass. There was so much hesitation in my steps, but I couldn't let another day pass without seeing the first woman that showed me *real* love. It had been five years since I graced this heartrending spot with my presence. The closer I got to the space, the tighter my chest became. I paused and took a few deep breaths to ease the pace of my heart.

"Come on, you can do this." I tried hard to convince myself everything was going to be okay. However, that was a boldfaced lie.

Finally, my feet moved forward and I was now standing in front of the headstone that read, *Brenda Riccardo. A loving and devoted wife and mother.* Beside her was my father, Fernando Riccardo. Tears immediately filled my eyes and I could no longer keep it in. They fell heavy, like a storm. The flowers I clutched in my hand were red roses, my mother's favorite. I placed them alongside the bench.

"Hey, beautiful. I've missed you so much." Removing my hoodie, I straddled the bench and placed both hands over her picture. Sadly, this was the only way I would ever touch her again. "It's been a while, but I'm here now and it'll be this way until I join you."

Unable to contain my emotions, I rocked uncontrollably, releasing the most horrid sound from the top of my lungs. "Whyyy? Why did you leave me? I would've helped you overcome everything we endured over the years. This is killing me, Ma."

Thinking about her untimely death broke my heart all over again and I felt like that teenage boy all over again.

"Ma, where you at?" I dropped my book bag on the floor and went into the kitchen.

Every day I got out of school, that's where she was waiting on me with a cold Pepsi and a beef patty from Charlie's Pastries. That was my go-to food until dinner was ready, but on this particular day, it wasn't there and I knew something was wrong. As I walked past the mantle, I noticed the wedding photo of my parents was missing. *A sudden feeling of trepidation took over my body and I scurried down the hallway in search for her.*

"Ma! Ma!" That scream was painful, as I searched for her in a panic.

Her bedroom door was locked, so I kicked it repeatedly until I knocked that bitch off the hinges, sending it crashing down to the floor. There was no amount of drugs or alcohol that could've numbed me for the gory scene in front my eyes. On instinct, I rushed to her side, cradling her head and silently praying I could save her, but deep down I knew I couldn't.

The one person that loved me unconditionally was laid out across the bed, with a medium sized hole in her temple. Her eyes were closed like she was sleeping. The blood was beginning to stiffen on the sheets. She had been dead a while now. In her arms, on top of her heart was the missing photo of her and my dad. Next to her, was a neatly written note addressed to me.

Brandon, my heart and world, please don't be upset with me for what I have done. My life that I knew on earth has been over ever since the day your father was murdered in front of my eyes. While I was on that sidewalk clutching him tightly in my arms, I watched him take his last breath and that took everything out of me. At that moment I died too, but I knew I couldn't leave you to fend for yourself in the system at a young age. You are a man now and I have raised you right, so I know you will make it on your own. Don't see this as goodbye forever, but a see you later instead.

Son, don't beat yourself up because there is nothing you could've done to prevent the inevitable. This was bound to happen and no, you didn't do anything wrong. The day you find your soulmate, you will never want to continue out life without them. I loved you with every breath in my body on earth and I still love you in death. Until we meet again, son, I love you forever.

Love, Mom

My vision was blurry from the fluid that blinded me. Leaning my head back, I blinked a few times and looked up at the sky. "I'm living good, baby, and you know I would've taken care of you without a doubt."

I dropped my head and dried my tears with my hand. "I came to let you know that Breanna is six years old now and she's getting so big, Ma. I wish she would've gotten the chance to meet you and see how wonderful you were."

The birds' chirping grabbed my attention, as I sat underneath the tree. I looked up to make sure none of them muthafuckas was trying to shit on me. I'll blast one of them shits and not think twice about it. For some reason, my thoughts made me laugh.

"Ma, I'm a loose cannon." I chuckled some more. "I met this amazing woman and she means so much to me. You said I would meet my soulmate one day and I think she's the one. Recently, I found out that we expecting a baby, so you gone be a grandma for the second time. I want to propose to her, but I believe that marriage changes people and I don't want to ruin what we have."

Reality settled in and I sighed. "But, that's not all. I killed her brother and it's killing me on the inside, knowing that I'm responsible for everything she's been going through. I want to be honest with her, but I can't risk losing her. I know if she finds out, she'll leave me and probably turn my ass in. I can't say I would blame her."

Zuri was everything I could ask for in a woman, and my biggest fear of committing to the next step, was that she would change on me for the worst. The last time I moved quickly, that shit turned out bad, but Zuri was different and I honestly didn't believe she would change on me. But now, I had a new fear. What if she found out I was the one that killed her brother? That question played out in my head every day.

"On a positive note, she didn't think I would be happy about the baby, but she's wrong. After she told me, I took her to meet Breanna and we all went out to dinner. That meant a lot in my eyes. I promised myself, I would never let anyone I had no intentions of being with for the long haul, meet my daughter."

Now on my feet, I looked down at her final resting place and forced a smile. It was hard because there was so much hate in my heart for the bitches that failed to help her when she was suffering. If only I was old enough and wise enough to read the signs, I could've saved her.

"Ma, I need you to watch over me and protect me from everything I'm about to do. With every passing day, my heart breaks and time doesn't heal all wounds. So, with that being said, I will be taking the law into my own hands. Every person that didn't help you will be right out here with you, and I promise you that. Those muthafuckas didn't care about me or you and that's why you here. I'm killin' them all, Ma. You probably not happy about what I'm saying, but this has to be done. I love you and I'll be back after I'm done being the undertaker."

Before I prepared to leave, I kissed my hand and placed it on top of her picture. "No matter what happens, you still my favorite girl. I just added two more to the bunch and possibly one more, if the baby is a girl. Continue being my angel."

Pulling the hoodie over my head, I walked off with the weight of the world on my shoulders. It was my job to make sure I avenged my mother's death and I was gone do just that.

***

Gucci

I was awakened from my nap by the chiming sound from my cell phone. At first, I wasn't going to answer it, but I had to just in case it was an emergency. Squinting my eyes, it was a number I recognized and I was glad I decided to pick up.

"Hello."

"Yes, hi, is this Mr. Marquez Williams?" the woman on the phone asked.

"Yes, it is." My heart was hitting against my chest like King Kong, being that I didn't know what to expect from this impromptu call. "How can I help you?"

"Sherry is speaking clearly and she's asking for you. Can you come down and see her?"

My energy level spiked to the max and I felt replenished suddenly. I jumped up from the couch, planting my feet so hard on the floor, I felt the echo. "Yes. Yes, I can."

"When can you come down?"

"I'm on my way. I'll be there in half an hour."

"Okay, great. I'll let her know."

"Thank you."

The news I received was so good, I ran to find Mehzani. The bathroom door was closed, so I knocked first.

"Come in," she yelled.

"Get dressed, we have to go."

"Where are we going?"

"Just get dressed and come on."

Fifteen minutes later after rushing her, we were on our way. Throughout the entire drive, Mehzani bugged me about where we were going, but I didn't tell her. Soon enough, she would have her answer. Just as I pulled up to the destination and parked the car, she started back with the questions.

"What are we doing here?" There was a confused look on her face.

"You'll see."

We checked in at the front desk and walked through the lobby, until we made it to the room. For months I had been waiting on this moment and I was happy as hell.

"Hi, son," she whispered, as soon I crossed the threshold.

Mehzani held onto my arm like a scared little girl. I knew she was confused as to why we were here and who we were here to see. She let go of my hand and took a seat in the leather chair against the wall. I walked up to my mother and gave her the biggest hug.

"I'm so happy to see you." My grip on her was extremely tight. The pain I held so deep slowly eased up just a little. A few happy teardrops crept from eyes. After a minute or so, I let her go.

"The nurse said she is surprised with my speedy recovery." Her voice was raspy and winded, but she continued. "She said for some people, it could take years to recover the way I did."

"Yeah, you have really surprised me," I admitted.

My mom leaned her head to the side, turning her attention away from me. "Marquez, who is that girl? I don't know her."

That fast, I had completely forgotten all about Mehzani. My head swiveled in her direction. "Bae, come here so I can introduce you." She bit her nails as she walked over nervously.

"This is Mehzani, my girlfriend."

"Girlfriend?" She was definitely puzzled.

A phony smile spread across her lips, as she extended her arms to Mehzani. I knew she wasn't happy because I saw that look too much growing up. My baby stepped in closer, extending her arms out as well to embrace her new mother-in-law.

"I'm Sherry. So, how long have you been screwing my son?" She smirked. "And what have you done to him, because he don't claim females, let alone introduce me to his slut of the week."

Mehzani snapped her head back in shock. "Excuse me?"

My mama was really trippin', so I had to straighten her with the quickness. "You off yo' meds or something? Why you talkin' to her like that? She ain't nothing like the girls I used to fuck with. That was dead-ass wrong for you to say and you know it."

"Baby, I'm sorry." She laid down and pulled the blankets up to her neck.

I wasn't a disrespectful son to my mother, but she was reaching and I was certain she hurt Mehzani's feelings. I didn't like that shit one bit and she knew I only spoke like that when she was out of pocket.

"I think these meds are making me act out. I'ma lay down now." She was lying her ass off, 'cause wasn't shit wrong with her. Just being nasty for no apparent reason.

My girl wasn't trying to hear that shit, so she walked off. I thought she was going to sit down, until she strolled past the chair and out the door.

"Happy now?" She went too far and I was irritated with her behavior. "The first time your words are clear and you would insult my girl like that. I can't believe you would do some shit like that. You owe her an apology too."

"I'm sorry."

"If this is how you gone treat her, then I might as well leave you in here." That wasn't the truth, but I needed her to know I was serious about my relationship.

"I'll apologize."

"Yeah, I know. In the meantime, relax so I can take care of everything and find out when you'll be able to come home."

"Okay," she said softly.

When I stepped out the room, I saw Mehzani wandering around at the end of the hallway. So, I went to check on her. Placing my arms around her, I kissed her cheek. "I'm sorry about that, baby. She ain't all there, so you have to excuse what she said."

"I'm ready to go," she replied.

"Okay, let me go and talk to the nurse and I'll be back."

"Okay."

The nurse informed me that after she has been cleared by her MD and physical therapist, she was more than welcome to go home. My only job was to make sure she continued to receive the proper therapy in order to complete the recovery stage. My mom was happy to hear the good news and she couldn't wait to get out of here. Little did she know, we were leaving in the next few weeks to start over completely.

Mehzani was exhausted and hungry, so we stopped by the rib shack to get some food on the way home. When I whipped up in my Camaro, the line was longer than a muthafucka.

"Damn, bae, this shit crowded as fuck." I looked towards the passenger seat.

"I know, but my mouth is tuned up for it."

"A'ight, let's get out."

The line moved quicker than expected, so we were able to place it within fifteen minutes. We sat at a table with an umbrella positioned above it.

"I'm really sorry for the shit my mama said to you, but she gone apologize."

Mehzani looked into my eyes for a few seconds before she responded. "You don't have to make her apologize for something she wanted to say. It's fine."

"Nah, that shit wasn't right and I don't like that. We are a couple and she needs to respect you, the same way you gone respect her. I can't have the most important women in my life feuding with each other."

I grabbed the hand she had resting on her thigh and held it. "Do it for me, baby, okay? I promise it won't happen again and I mean that."

She thought for a minute, then she finally smiled. "For you, baby, I will."

"Thank you." I kissed her hand. "I love you."

Mehzani's eyes lit up the surrounding area. I had never said those words to her. "What?" The wrinkles in her forehead surfaced, as she placed her other hand on her chest. "You love me?"

"That's what I said."

"Aww, baby, I love you too." She leaned forward and our lips connected, with no regard to the people amongst the crowd.

After waiting for about twenty-five minutes, they finally called my name. "About time. Let's go."

We headed over to the crowd and a loud familiar laugh caught my attention, but I kept it moving. The last thing I needed was to bring attention in my direction. That shit didn't last long though.

"People act funny when they get lil' girlfriends and shit." Deja laughed out loud.

I ignored her and grabbed the food from the window, so we could get back to the car. Hopefully, this bitch didn't start no shit out here in public. Deja knew how to take you over the edge with that reckless-ass mouth of hers. As we walked past her, I peeped her expression from the corner of my eye.

"Damn, Gucci, so you gone walk past without saying shit to me?"

There she go with the bullshit, but I ignored her and kept walking. Mehzani didn't. "Who is that?"

"Nobody," I replied.

"I wasn't nobody last week," Deja spoke up and walked in our direction. "Tell her who I am, Gucci."

"Man, get the fuck outta here. You love drama wit'cho ratchet ass."

"You wasn't worried about me being ratchet when I was bouncing on that dick last week." Deja was loud and over the top.

"You a dumb-ass bitch, I swear." I opened the car door and looked at Mehzani, who was in turn eyeing me down with a death stare, but I simply didn't pay that any mind. "Get in the car."

Mehzani's face was stricken with pain. "You fucked her last week, Gucci?"

Not a single word fell from my lips. My intention was to never hurt her and I did the exact opposite. Now I regretted linking up with that trifling-ass bitch. "Bae, get in the car please," I pleaded.

"No. I need an answer before I go anywhere with you and I'm not playing with you." She folded her arms and stood outside the door.

"It was a mistake. We had some business together, but she had other plans when I got there."

"Stop lying to that girl." Deja stood at the front of the car. "He know we met up to fuck. We been fucking for years, so don't let his lying ass fool you."

I swear I was two seconds from slapping that ho' down and Mehzani was just standing there listening to the shit.

"Bae, get in the car and let's go, or you can stay here with her. We'll discuss this shit at the house." Mehzani finally got in the car and closed the door.

"Fuck you and that flock head ho'," Deja screamed, while standing in front of the car.

I rolled down the window. "Get the fuck out the way before I hit yo' dumb ass."

Deja didn't move at first, so I revved up the engine and that made her jump to the side. Hitting the gas, I turned the wheel in her direction and I felt a bump, followed by a scream.

"Ouuuuch! You ran my foot over, dumb-ass nigga," Deja screamed before falling to the ground.

"Fuck you and yo' foot, ho'," I shouted out the window then burned rubber, pulling off.

Mehzani ignored me during the entire ride home. The only thing that could be heard was her sniffling. The hurt she endured couldn't be taken away, but I had to do something to earn her trust again. I fucked up big time with this one.

By the time we made it to my apartment in Nexus by Sawgrass, she had stopped crying. I parked the car and turned off the engine. There was going to be a whole lot to explain to her. Just thinking about it gave me a headache.

"Mezhani, please talk to me." I sighed heavily. "I have a lot to explain to you. The story is much deeper than you think."

To my surprise, she gave me direct eye contact. In such a short time span, her eyes were red and puffy.

"You don't owe me an explanation, Gucci. I'm leaving you, so you can keep those 'I'm sorry' speeches to yourself. Thank you."

Mezhani got out the car and slammed my door hard enough to knock that bitch off the hinges. I watched as she speed walked through the parking lot into the darkness.

"Fuck!" I exclaimed, punching the steering wheel hard as fuck, wishing it was that bitch Deja's face instead.

Chapter 7

Zuri

With each passing day, the pain was not easier to bear, so whoever said that was a damn lie. Some days, I felt like throwing in the towel, but I had my precious baby growing inside of me. Therefore, I had to do my best and keep my unborn child safe and free from stress. Just thinking back to that day made me smile.

The second Brick announced he was happy about the pregnancy, I was so relieved. A tremendous weight had been lifted from my shoulders. After he left me for the second time, I just knew it was over for good. A few days later, I noticed some weird changes with my body. Things I never felt before and it made me nervous. I didn't know what to think. So, earlier that day, I decided to take a pregnancy test and it came back positive. It was crazy how he appeared right after I found out. That made me think we have a special telepathic connection or something.

That night, he took me out we picked up his daughter and it made me feel special that he introduced me to her, after stating that was something he didn't do. From the time I met her, I fell in love instantly. Breanna was the sweetest and cutest little girl with big brown eyes. Her complexion was brown and she wore her hair in two big afro puffs. I was certain that's how our little girl was going to look if we had one. Breanna wasn't shy by a long shot, she warmed up to me quickly and asked so many questions about me and her daddy. If I didn't know any better, I would say her mother coached her ahead of time.

Normally on Sundays, I would lay around and watch Lifetime all day, but today was different for me. If I wanted to be the best mother humanly possible, I needed to clean out the skeletons in my closet that were racked up to the ceiling. And, start healing from the loss of my brother. Thanks to me being so distraught at the funeral, I allowed Mehzani to get away, but I wasn't going to stop until I found her. For ten minutes, I sat in the car just staring at the building in front of me, with uncertainty in my heart and tears in my eyes. I was unsure about carrying my dirt inside the house of the Lord. Afraid he would wonder why a sinner like me had the audacity to grace his holy establishment.

"Lord, if you don't want me here, I will leave. Just give me a sign that it's okay to stay." My head fell onto the steering wheel. "Please, God, help me."

It wasn't a full minute later that I heard a tap on my window. Slowly, I raised my head to see an older lady staring at me, so I quickly wiped my eyes and rolled down my window.

"Hello," my voice cracked.

"Are you okay, honey?"

"Yes, ma'am," I lied.

"You know we don't hold service outside?" She chuckled and adjusted the big hat on her head. Subconsciously, I giggled. "That's better, come on the inside. You can hear the word much better in there."

"I don't think I should with the baggage I'm bringing in. The Lord may not want me in there with all this foolishness on my heart."

"Nonsense. No one in that building is perfect. You are his child and he accepts you for who you are. It took strength for you to come here and acknowledge your faults, so let's go and Ms. Ella will not take no for an answer."

I was surprised when she pulled my car door open and placed her hands on her hip. "I'm waiting."

That was the sign I asked for, so I turned the car off and grabbed my keys and purse. I took a deep breath before I got out the car and closed the door. My knees buckled as I walked alongside Ms. Ella into the sanctuary. There was a male usher standing at the door, smiling.

"Good morning, Sister Ella and guest." He handed us a program.

"Good morning," we both replied.

"Go on in, you're right on time."

"See you after service for the dinner." He nodded his head and escorted us to a half-full bench.

The church members were all standing, singing and clapping to the music. Ms. Ella made her way inside and I was near the aisle. She sat her purse on the pew and joined in. Not me, I couldn't wait to sit down. I wasn't ready for any type of participation just yet. I had to warm up first. Ms. Ella looked down at me and waved her hand for me to stand. I really didn't want to, but I did it. It wasn't like I knew the song, so I just stood in place fighting the spirit that was trying its best to get ahold of me. After standing there looking lost for five minutes, the choir played a song I recognized, Hezekiah Walker, "Every Praise", but I still remained silent.

Throughout the entire church, all you could hear is people singing, "Every praise is to our God, every word of worship with one accord." The devil was winning with me, as I continued to fight the feeling inside of me. Ms. Ella looked at me with a warm smile, singing her heart out and pointed in front of us. I followed her hand and saw what she was trying to show me. Up on the wall above the pulpit, was a screen with the lyrics on it. The more I watched everyone enjoy the healing spirituals, the more I wanted to join in. My feet started to move first and so did my arms. Before I knew it, I was rocking side to side, clapping, allowing the music to take over my body. It felt good to loosen up and let the spirit take over my body. Soon after, I was singing my heart out and the tears were flowing heavily, as if I was at a funeral. And, technically it was. I was burying the old Zuri and giving birth to a new and improved one.

Every praise is to our God. Every word of worship with one accord every praise every praise is to our God. Sing hallelujah to our God Glory hallelujah is due our God every praise every praise is to our God. (Hey this is what I love) God my Savior God my Healer God my Deliverer Yes He is, yes He is.

One of the ushers walked up and handed me a few tissues. I was crying my eyes out and it was so therapeutic to my soul. It felt like the tears were cleansing my body and washing away my sins. The song lasted another five minutes and the music came to an end.

When the pastor began to speak, we all took our seats in preparation for the sermon.

"Will the church say Amen?"

"Amen," we repeated.

"We giving all the praises to God this morning. Hallelujah."

The congregation shouted, "Amen," on one accord.

"God woke all of us up this morning and gave us the ability to get up and make it here for praise and worship. I feel so good this morning, I felt like running to church."

The pastor laughed and so did the church. That made me giggle as well. I couldn't remember the last time I stepped foot in a church besides Legend's funeral, and I knew the Lord frowned that day at the way I showed up and out. Aside from that, the only other time was for another funeral about four years ago. A neighborhood friend of mine was killed in a head-on collision and seeing her laid up in that casket did something to my young soul. All I kept thinking was it could've been me.

One night, we left a hotel party around one in the morning and just like any eighteen-year old, we had a few drinks. Kesha was supposed to be riding with me, but there was a guy she liked named Marcus, so she did everything she could do to get his attention. When the party was over, they all wanted to go to the beach, but I didn't want to go, so I declined the offer and rode home with another friend of mine. The next morning, I got a call saying Marcus lost control of the car on the highway and ran head-on into the wall, killing everybody in the vehicle. That broke my heart in so many pieces, because we did everything together. After their funerals, I made a promise to God to attend church, which lasted for about a month before I stopped.

Throughout the sermon, over the past hour and a half, I was in and out on the word. My mind was all over the place, as I reflected back on my actions in life that put me in the predicament I was in at that moment. All I wanted was a redo, so I could start fresh with a second chance at life.

"I want to speak to all of you in here today. Every person in this room has been through some things. I've been through some too. Some of us just hide it better than others."

Those words pulled me in and he had my undivided attention. "Some of you in here are struggling with self- esteem issues, financial burdens, health issues, drug abuse, alcohol abuse and relationship issues. Many have been molested, violated in some way and you struggling to find a way to forget about it, but y'all don't hear me though."

"Amen, Pastor," Ms. Ella shouted and raised her hand high to the ceiling. "They don't hear you. Say it louder for the ones in the back."

The pastor took a sip of water and wiped his forehead with his handkerchief. My eyes never left him because this sermon was dedicated especially for me. I knew there was a reason I showed up. As he spoke to my soul, I rubbed my hand over my belly. The steps I was taking was all for my little one growing inside of me.

"You have to let go and let God. Forgive them for doing wrong towards you and remember that you doing it for you and not them. They gone on about their life, while you still living in misery. I'm here to tell you that stops today, beloved."

The pastor then stepped down onto the floor, front and center. "To all my visitors looking for a church home, we welcome you with open arms. Come on down and let's start your healing process. If you have to go in a coma to think about it, then this ain't for you, but if you reached your breakthrough, then get up here. Come to Jesus up on this altar. He's waiting on you. God wants to deliver you and remove every burden that has been placed on your heart. He wants to give you a new start and erase that shame and guilt you are feeling. Get right with Jesus today, because tomorrow ain't prom-ised."

My body was glued to my seat and I could not move whatsoever, so I just sat there and watched three people walk to the front. Fear-stricken, I remained in my seat, praying for the strength to speak up. Ms. Ella looked at me and it made me miss my own grandmother.

"Go on up there, you made it this far."

"I'm scared."

Ms. Ella grabbed my hand and stood up. "I'll walk with you."

My trembling lips formed into a nervous smile, as I nodded my head. "Okay."

As we walked hand in hand, down the aisle people began to stare and all I wanted to do was run and be one with the wind. Even though I was completely covered from head to toe, I felt naked and cold. Shame, guilt and embarrassment hung on my face like a Halloween mask. Their crucifying stares pierced my soul and I felt as if they could see all of the dirt I did in my life.

Ms. Ella let go of my hand when I was just a few feet away from the pastor. *There goes that damn buckling of my knees again, hopefully no one could hear them*, I thought. The man of the cloth walked up to me.

"What's your name?"

"Zuri," I replied.

The pastor traced my forehead with oil in the shape of a cross. "Father God, today I give you Zuri. Take over her body and make her whole again. Your child needs you. She's broken and crying on the inside. Her bravery to stand in front of faces she's never seen before and give her life to you, speaks volumes. Deliver her from whatever is weighing her down. Give her the strength she needs to heal and get over that hurt. Allow her to walk by faith and not by sight. In Jesus name we pray, Amen."

After the service was over, I felt like a new woman and thanked Ms. Ella for that. She gave me her phone number and told me not to hesitate to call her. Even it was in the wee hours of the morning. My soul had been delivered and I was ready to face the storm. I was in a good mood and no one could knock me down. A celebratory dinner was necessary, so I opted to make oxtails, rice, cabbage, cornbread and macaroni and cheese. Brick was gone be happy about that. I got into my car and connected my Bluetooth. The Holy Ghost still had a hold on me and I was in the mood to hear some gospel. Thumbing through my phone, I went to YouTube and found a song special to my heart.

"Hold on and don't give up. Don't you worry, you don't have to cry, 'cause he, he sees what you're going through, yes, yes he does." I slid my Dolce and Gabbana shades over my eyes and pulled off.

Destiny Skai

Chapter 8

Brick

Zuri and I were lying in bed, watching some movie called *Bride of a Hustla* on YouTube and relaxing after all that damn food we ate. I don't know what church did to her, but if she was gone throw down like that afterwards, then she needed to go every Sunday and Bible study on Wednesdays shit. My phone started ringing, but I ignored it. My Sundays were on special reserve for my lady. If a muhfucka didn't get robbed or killed, that shit could wait until Monday morning and I don't mean after midnight. That means after 8:00 am, when I start my day.

"Oh shit, this was filmed in Deepside. I know them townhouses from anywhere. Why you ain't tell me this was filmed in the hometown?"

"I told you, but I guess you wasn't paying attention."

"Who made this?"

"A girl from here." She half-ass answered my damn question.

"No shit, Sherlock. What's her name?"

"Destiny Skai. She write books too. This movie is actually based on the book."

"Oh, yeah. I used to read a lot of books when I was in the feds. Not sure if I read anything by her though. I read some books by this nigga name Ca$h. That nigga lit with the pen. He had to really live the shit he write about."

"I read *Restraining Order* by him." She smiled a little too hard.

"Why you cheesing so damn hard? That's yo' author crush or some shit? I know how y'all women get."

"No. That man can be my daddy."

That last comment almost made me say something about her pervert-ass daddy, but I let that shit slide. Her ass probably liked old niggas anyway. She better not let me see her lusting over any nigga in the free world or the penitentiary. Zuri had me fucked up on every level.

"You need to read *'Til My Casket Drops,* so you can be my Keedy that shit straight fie. A real ride or die chick."

"I'll read that if you read *The Fetti Girls.* Now, Blacque Barbee is the baddest. She don't fuck off period." There was so much excitement in her voice.

"Blacque Barbee?" My brow shifted downward. "It has lips on the cover?"

"Yeah," she replied.

"Oh, hell yeah. I read all three of those. Dem shits was lit as fuck. Barbee sounded finer than a bitch. Now that's what she need to turn into a movie."

"I agree."

My phone rang again and I still wasn't about to answer it. When it stopped, they called back two more times, so I figured it was urgent.

"That must be one of your hoes, blowing up yo' shit like that." Zuri seemed bothered by the fact I didn't want to answer something I paid the bill on.

"Hush. I don't have ho's and I been told you that."

"Well, pick it up if you have nothing to hide. You screen everything I do, so now I'm doing it to you."

"I keep telling you that I'm the man in this relationship and you steady forgetting that." To close her mouth, I rolled over and grabbed it from the nightstand. "Yo' ass went to church this morning and the devil still in you. That's a damn shame." I checked the screen before showing it to her. "It's my baby mama homegirl."

"The Lord knows my heart and what the hell she keeps calling you for?" Zuri snapped.

"I don't know." That was the truth, because I really didn't know why she ringing my shit off the hook. We were cool from back in the day, and she was the one who hooked me up with Deja's funky ass.

"Let me see." I showed her jealous ass the phone, so she could see the name *Erin (Sis)*, displayed on the screen before I answered.

"What up, sis?" I put the phone on speaker since I had nothing to hide.

"You not busy, are you? I need to holla at 'chu about some shit."

"I'm chillin' wit' my lady, but go 'head."

"Last night I was at the rib shack with Deja and we saw Gucci up there with his chick. At first, I thought she was just fuckin' with him to make his girl mad, but then I realized she was dead-ass serious."

"About what?" None of this shit was making sense and I wanted her to get straight to the point.

"Deja really confronted this man about being with a female and not speaking to her. Gucci called her ratchet."

I couldn't help but laugh. "That ho is ratchet."

"Yeah, but after he said that she was like, I wasn't ratchet last week when we was fuckin'."

When she said that shit, I stopped laughing right away. It was no longer a laughing matter to hear my first cousin, the nigga I grew up with, was hittin' my baby mama. True enough, I didn't give a fuck who she fucked, but my cousin, hell nah. That ho' could've fucked my homeboy and I wouldn't give several fucks.

"What?" I shouted.

"Yeah, that's what I said too. Then, she told that girl him and her had been fuckin' for years. Bruh, on everything, I would've never hooked you up with her if I knew that."

"It's all good. It ain't yo' fault she a ho'."

"That's why I had to call you, just in case y'all was still smashing."

"Hell nah. I ain't smash Deja since I came home and that was only once. After that, I never touched her again." Zuri was staring dead in my mouth, listening for all details.

"Well, good. I can't believe she so damn nasty. You can tell her I told you. I don't care 'cause it needed to be told."

"It's all good, sis. Ion name drop, but I'ma hit you up later. I need some answers."

"Okay."

When I hung up and looked over at Zuri, she was looking me dead in the face. I'm sure in her mind she had questions, so I beat her to the questionnaire she was about to hit me with sooner or later.

"Before you say anything, I don't feel no type of way about her, but that's some foul shit to fuck my cousin and that's real talk. If you don't understand that, then I don't know what to tell you. My daughter over there, so I need to find out what's been going on in my absence while I was locked up."

Zuri placed her hand on her arm. "I understand and I wasn't going to say anything about that, 'cause you deserve to know. I'm not selfish like that."

Sincerity was in her voice, so I believed her. If she was lying, I couldn't tell. "That's why I love you."

I pecked her on those soft ass lips that were constantly wrapped around my wood. "Come on, let's make this pop-up visit. When I speak I need to witness the lies roll off her tongue, so I can punch them shits back down her throat. She won't be hanging up the phone today."

"Just don't kill her."

***

Zuri and I stood on Deja's porch as I banged hard on her door, waiting on her to open it. My first mind told me to kick that muthafucka in like the feds did me, but I wanted to save my energy for this foot I was about to put in her ass. The locks clicked on the door and my right hand instantly started to twitch. I was itching to slap the fuck out of this trifling slut bucket. Deja's baldhead ass snatched the door open and rolled her neck with an attitude.

"Why you banging on my door like you pay rent at my shit? And, you had the nerve to bring company."

"Ho', shut up. If it wasn't for Section-8, it wouldn't be yo' shit."

Deja folded her arms across her chest. "Whatever, I'm not about to entertain you. What do you want?"

"I'll buy all these shits and evict yo' punk ass."

"What the fuck do you want, Brick?" She placed her hand the doorknob like she was about to close it.

"Back up and let me in. I ain't on this fuck shit today." She knew better, so she backed the fuck up. I grabbed Zuri's hand and pulled her inside. "Where the fuck is my daughter?"

"In the room. Why?" she yelled.

"Zuri, go back there and get her." I pointed in the direction of my princess' room.

"Wha—"

Deja was ready to talk shit, but I cut her off and stepped up closely, glaring down in her face. "She don't need to witness none of this."

"Witness what?"

"So, you was fucking Gucci while I was locked up and before I went in, huh?"

"I-I mean. What?" She backed up to put distance in between us.

"I know playing dumb is your forte, but don't try me. A slick can't outslick a slicker. You know what the fuck I'm talkin' 'bout."

"Well, don't ask me shit that you already know the answer to."

Sarcasm never sat well with me. Her words made my blood boil. The rage I felt triggered my left hand and I could feel my fingertips tremble. I pursed up my lips, but I couldn't keep calm. Quickly, I raised my hand.

Whap!

The sound of skin cracking like a bullwhip echoed throughout the living room. Deja stumbled backwards and collapsed onto the couch, clutching the side of her face.

"You so fuckin' stupid."

"For fuckin' wit' you, I am." I scurried in her direction with my fist balled up and the noise behind me stopped me dead in my tracks.

"Daddy!" my baby girl screeched.

Quickly suppressing my anger, I turned to face her. "Hey, baby." When I knelt down, she ran up and hugged my neck.

"I missed you. Am I going with you and Zuri?" My heart melted, as I stared in her big brown eyes. Breanna never saw me yell before and I never wanted her to witness that side of me.

"Yes, baby."

"Okay. I need to get my clothes." She bounced up and down in excitement.

"That's okay. We'll go shopping." I placed my hand on her shoulder. "Baby, go outside with Zuri. I need to talk to your mother okay?"

"Okay, Daddy." Breanna turned on her heels and grabbed Zuri by the hand. "Come on. Let's go outside and wait on Daddy."

Zuri smiled. "Okay." Then, she looked at me with a disapproving look. "Remember what I told you."

I nodded my head and waited on them to go outside. As soon as the door closed I turned back to face the bitch that I thought loved me.

"So, you don't have shit to say?" My chest heaved up and down.

"What do you want me to say, Brick?" She was still holding the side of her face.

"I want to hear it from the horse's mouth." Erin's word was enough for me to believe it, but it also confirmed what Playa said the night I took him out.

"Yes. We slept together one time by accident before you went in, and the other times just happened because he was over here a lot, helping me with Breanna."

That bullshit excuse made my eyebrows furrow. "Fucking ain't no goddam accident. You had plenty of time to think while you was gettin' butt-ass naked for that nigga. Both of y'all bitches triflin', but it's all good. I ain't trippin' off no ho' or the fact that you had his son and pinned it on another nigga."

I paused for a split second, kneading my forehead. My thoughts were all over the place. "So, is Breanna my daughter?"

"For real? You questioning her now?" Deja sat up on the couch and starred at me, as the tears welled up in her eyes.

I wasn't fazed by crocodile tears that ain't mean shit. My eyes scanned the room in search of her phone. "You damn right. I don't trust you or that grimy ass nigga. We share the same bloodline and we resemble, so I don't know who her daddy is."

"You know she's your daughter."

"I don't know shit, so just gimme your phone." She pulled it from her pocket and handed it to me. "We about to find out."

"What you finna do?"

"Nah, you finna call and question him about last night." I scrolled through her call log and found his number. "Y'all still fuckin' too." Shaking my head, I hit send and put it on speaker. Then, I looked at her to give a fair warning, before passing her the phone.

"You better not say shit out the way or I will punch yo' ass dead in the mouth. Try me if you think I'm playing. All I wanna know is if my daughter belong to me."

"What am I supposed to say?"

"Figure it out. Y'all was out here playing house and shit. So, you know exactly what to say."

***

Gucci

Mehzani and I sat down and discussed what happened between me and Deja last night. If I wanted things to work out, I knew that I had to be honest and lay it out on the table. No matter how bad it sounded falling out my mouth. The hardest part was revealing something I never told anyone, not even Mel, but I had to tell her just in case this shit went viral and the speculations surfaced.

In Lauderdale, gossip spread like a wildfire and these bitches and niggas loved to put shit on Facebook. They were disrespectful with it. A while ago, somebody recorded a nigga bleeding to death from a gunshot wound. That was some foul shit. I prayed on the daily that if I was gunned down by one of these fuck niggas, no one recorded me dying for my loved ones to see.

The look in Mehzani's eyes hurt my soul, because I hurt her deeply. They were glassy, but a tear never escaped her lids. Those were never my intentions and I should've never let Deja get in the way of what I was trying to build. "You know I was prepared to walk away from you for good?"

"I know it's gone take a while for me to gain back your trust, but I'm willing to do anything to get it back. I can't say I'm sorry enough, but I'll never do it again and that's my promise."

"You get one more chance to prove that to me. If it happens again, I'm leaving for good and I won't think twice about it." She sighed. "I have one question for you though."

"Shoot." I nodded my head.

"If I was the one that cheated, would you have forgiven me?"

She hit me with a tough one, but I already knew the answer to that question. "Honestly." I paused for a few seconds. "Probably not."

"Well, that's a double standard don't you think?" Her brow shifted downward in confusion.

"It may seem that way, but there are different expectations for men and women. You are expected to remain faithful no matter what. No man wants a woman that sleeps around."

Mehzani held her hand up. "Hold up! Hold the fuck up. So, tell me again why you slept with Deja? 'Cause clearly she was sleeping around and you didn't have a problem with that."

Just as I was about to answer, my cell started ringing. The number was no longer saved, but I recognized the number right away and the disgust must have showed on my face.

"Who is that?" Mehzani's face was scrunched up to the max.

"The chick that thinks she had the baby from me." I sat there eyeing the phone, not wanting to answer it. Her timing was all fucked up. I was trying to make amends with my lady and here she go with the bullshit.

"What the fuck does she want?" I frowned, mumbling under my breath.

"Well, answer it. It might be important." Mehzani crossed her legs and sat her hands in her lap.

"Hell no, I ain't fuckin' wit' her ass no mo'." The phone went to voicemail, but she called right back.

"Gucci just pick up the damn phone, unless you have more to hide. Just see what the bitch wants or I'm leaving." Mehzani's tone was filled with a lot of agitation, so I picked up to keep us from arguing once again.

"What do you want, man?" I snapped, putting the phone to my ear.

"Gucci!" she yelled.

"What?" my voice matched hers.

"This Deja."

"Man, what the fuck do you want?"

"Brick is questioning me about Breanna and about my son. What did you tell him, because I don't know what to say?"

"I ain't tell him shit. So, why the fuck you callin' me? You made it very clear that you wanted me to stay away when you had her. I asked you if there was a possibility and you said no. I did my part when he was gone, so leave me out of that. I'm just her uncle."

There was some scuffling on the other end of the phone and then I heard Brick in the background. "Nigga, you was fucking my baby mama all along, huh?"

"Bitch, you had me on speaker?" That was some straight-up bullshit. "Bruh, it wasn't even like that. Man, shit just went left when I was over there checking on her and Breanna."

"Nigga, you fucked her before I went in. She done already told me 'bout y'all, so miss me wit' the fuck shit."

My body sprung upwards like he was standing in my living room and I needed to defend myself. "Bruh, let's just talk about this." I paced the floor. "Damn, this wasn't supposed to happen like this. We family, man, let's sit down and talk about this."

Brick laughed. "This coming from the same fuck-ass nigga that turned his back on me when my mom passed away. You and yo' pussy-ass mammy."

"Damn, that's fucked up. I guess family don't mean shit to you?"

"Hell no!" Brick yelled so loudly through the phone I had to move it from my ear. "Fuck family. Y'all ain't give a fuck about a nigga when my old girl passed. The whole family left me for dead. All y'all muhfuckas dead to me."

Brick was talking mad greasy, but I needed him to know that he wasn't the only one with ill feelings. "My nigga, you been dead to me and that's why I was fucking yo' chick. And, you got my ole girl hooked on drugs. Yeah nigga, she told me all about it when she thought she was dying, but if you got something to get off yo' chest, you know where to find me."

I hung the phone up and tossed it on the couch because I was done talking to him. He didn't want this built-up pressure. The shit he did to my mama was unwarranted. It was funny knowing we had the same blood running through our veins. When I snapped out of it, Mehzani was looking at me like I was crazy. I was on ten and needed a drink to calm myself down. I got up and headed for the kitchen.

Chapter 9

Brick

After hearing the shit Gucci said to her, I was ready to bury that bitch six feet in the dirt and not funeral style. That was too easy, I wanted to do the burial myself. My blood felt hot running through my veins. Just the thought of my baby not belonging to me hurt a nigga heart. I been there since day one. Attended every doctor's appointment, the birth, signed the birth certificate and I witnessed every first thing she did until I got jammed up. Even then my role in her life never wavered and I made sure she was taken care of from behind the wall.

"So, after all this time Breanna may not be mine, huh?" I bit down hard on my lip. The coppery tasting fluid hit my tongue, causing me to swallow.

Deja just sat there staring at me with those fake-ass tears in her eyes. Then she started rocking back and forth, sobbing. "I'm sorry. It was a mistake. Just like the one you made."

The fact that she had to bring up the past and remind me that I cheated first was her guilty conscience. What she did was no accident, but a clear sign of revenge and for that, she was gone have to pay the piper. Women in relationships had no business cheating. I don't give a fuck what he did. That was a different ball game. A man's value didn't depreciate because of the amount of females he slept with. That only applied to women and her mammy should've taught her that, but hell she ain't no better.

"Bullshit," I yelled, as I kicked the coffee table with my foot causing her to jump.

"That type of shit doesn't just happen. You made that decision. So, when did y'all start fuckin'?" Slow stroking my beard, I thought back to a time when it could've happened. "Was it the night you didn't come home after you found out about Dana? And, don't lie to me. You will only make it worst on yourself."

Her eyes shifted to the floor and I knew I hit that shit dead on the head. "Yes, but Brick, I swear I didn't plan on it happening. That night when I caught y'all leaving the hotel, I was drunk and I wasn't thinking straight."

"That's very interesting now. As a matter of fact, how did you find us?"

"Gucci told me."

As I thought back to that night, it made me laugh. That punk-ass nigga set me up from the jump and snitched on my ass. She wasn't lying. Gucci was the only one that knew I was with Dana. I always had a feeling he wanted to fuck her. Any time me and Deja got into it, his bitch ass was always on her side.

"Y'all planned that shit."

"No, I swear I didn't know."

"You lyin' or that nigga set yo' dumb ass up so he can fuck. Either way you fell for the shit. That was a weak ho' move. You wasn't down for a nigga in the first place. How you let another nigga tell you somethin' 'bout yo' nigga?"

"Brick, I still love you and I'm sorry." Deja acted as if she was so hurt making all that damn noise. She was boo-hoo crying, making snot bubbles and all.

"Stop saying that shit, because you don't. You only loved what I did for you. You was a fuckin' gold digger and still is."

"That's not fair, don't do that. Are you forgetting that I was working, but you wanted me to be a stay at home mom? You wanted me to depend on you." Deja was breathing hard, but she kept talking. "I didn't want to have a baby in the first place and that's why I tried to abort her by drinking vinegar, bleach, and carrying heavy-ass boxes."

My ears couldn't believe what the fuck I was hearing and now all the times she was sick made perfectly good sense. That ho' tried to kill my baby. The next thing I knew, I pounced on that bitch like I was a lion and she was a gazelle. My body was on top of hers in a straddling position, choking the life out of her. At any given moment, I could pop her neck like a Popsicle stick. Deja tried to claw her way from my grip, but I was way too strong.

"Bitch, I took care of you. I did everything for you and you had the nerve to fuck this nigga and try to kill my daughter? Ho', I should kill you."

Deja tried to scream, but nothing would come out. My hands held onto her throat like a pair of vice grips. She kicked her legs tirelessly until she got tired of fighting and gave up.

**

Deja

My lungs were starting to burn, as they desperately fought for air. Little dark spots blinded my vision. My life flashed before my eyes and I could slowly feel myself fading in and out of consciousness. In between the flashes, I saw Breanna's beautiful face with the puffy cheeks. I loved her to death, despite the attempts I took to get rid of her, so I had to fight for my life. I tried kicking my legs harder in hopes he would let go, but he didn't. There was no escape from Brick's deadly hands. The same hands he used to comfort me were the same hands trying to end my life. The fight was slowly leaving my body. I gave up and just laid there. If I was to die right now, I knew my baby would be well taken care of. And, maybe she was better off without me.

My eyes fluttered and tears ran from the sides of both eyes. Deep down inside I was hoping that his girlfriend came back inside. If he saw Breanna, I knew he would stop. Before he went in and we would argue and fight, he would never allow our baby girl to see the bad side of him. Brick stopped abruptly and I was finally free. I could breathe again. Hungrily, I inhaled all the air I could gather in a short span of time.

Brick grabbed me by the hair and that confirmed the fight wasn't over. "Brick, stop please." My voice was hoarse, making it hard to get the sound out. "I'm begging you."

"Fuck you." He applied all of his weight onto my small frame and punched me with a closed fist in my nose. Several more punches followed. I covered my face and curled up into the fetal position, with my face pressed deep into the couch cushion. I wasn't about to fight back because I knew it would only get worse, so I laid there helpless, confused and hurt. He had never put his hands on me like that, so I was in total shock. The most he ever did was slap and rough my ass up a little bit. Not damn near bludgeon me to death.

The beating seemed as if it lasted for hours, but I knew it had only been a few minutes. Brick pounded on me a few more times before coming to a complete stop. I waited until he walked away before I sat up on the sofa. My nose was bleeding heavily. My shirt was soaked in blood, but I was too afraid to even go to the bathroom. Instead, I just sat there applying pressure to my nose, using my shirt.

Brick emerged from the back room with Breanna's favorite doll. He paused and there was this evil ass look in his eyes.

"You better get on yo' knees and pray to God that's my daughter. If not, yo' ass will be buried or my name ain't muthafuckin' Brandon Brick Riccardo."

That was the last thing he said to me before he walked out the door. I managed to lift myself from the sofa and wobble to the bathroom. My body was sore and I was certain that my nose was broken. I flicked on the light and gaped, as I glanced in the mirror. My face brought me to tears and eventually, down to my knees. The fight was over, but the pain had been kicked into full gear. He was about to make my life a living hell and there was nothing I could do about it. Brick was officially a man scorned and I was to blame.

"God, please let Breanna be his daughter. Please," I cried. "I just don't know." If I didn't know anything else in life, I knew he didn't make idle threats and he would make good on his promise.

Chapter 10

Brick

On my way down the sidewalk, I stopped and placed Breanna's American Girl doll between my knees. Then, I took off the shirt I was wearing and balled it up. That bitch got blood on my shit and I didn't want Zuri or Breanna to see it, but of course, I could see her big ass eyes through the window. She didn't hide the fact that she was eye balling me hard as hell. It was hard to shake the anger, but I had to pretend and go into daddy mode. Taking the doll back into my hand I took long strides, so I could get out of Dodge. The car was running, so I hopped in, dropped the doll in the seat and pulled off without looking in her direction.

"What did you do?" Zuri's voice was soft and sweet, making it hard to resist conversation. Before responding, I looked in the rearview to see what my baby was doing. I observed her rocking in the seat, smiling as she played with Zuri's phone.

"She can't hear us. I have her watching a movie." She then leaned sideways in the seat, awaiting my answer. "Now, what did you do?"

"I kept my promise and didn't kill her." That was the truth, but she was in bad shape.

"That's blood on your shirt?"

"Yeah." I took a quick glance at her while trying to keep my eyes on the road. "I bust her nose."

"Give me your shirt." Zuri extended her hand over to the driver side, so I passed it to her. Quickly taking a peek at Breanna, she tossed it into her purse and zipped it up.

"You think she gone call the police?"

My eyes remained on the road as I zipped through traffic before I missed my turn. "Deja a lot of thangs, but crazy ain't one of them."

Zuri sucked her teeth. "Yeah okay, if you say so. She was crazy enough to cheat with your cousin. I wouldn't put shit past her."

"I'm glad you find the humor in this shit. My pain ain't no laughing matter," I snapped.

That was a sensitive ass subject and now wasn't the time to crack no fuckin' jokes. If she was any other broad, I would've slapped them slick words back down her throat. Zuri was lucky I loved her ass with my whole heart and I just couldn't see myself putting my hands on her.

"I'm sorry, baby, and I didn't laugh." She grabbed my hand and rubbed it gently. "I'm just saying, don't put it past her."

The situation was making me snap on my baby when I knew she meant no harm. Moving my hand, I took ahold of her hand and brought it up to my mouth and kissed it. "No, I'm sorry. Her bullshit got me so pissed off that I'm not thinking straight, so I understand what you saying."

"It's okay, baby. I understand your frustration, but I'm here for you, so don't worry about anything."

It felt good to know Zuri was really down for a nigga. I couldn't remember the last time I had a female that was here genuinely. Someone not infatuated with my street cred or money. This relationship was different and it made me want to work on dealing with my anger, but only when it came to her. Zuri was close to having me wrapped around her finger and of course, I wasn't about to tell her. The moment I did that, would be the day I gave her an inch and she'd take a foot. Not on my watch.

We finally made it back to Zuri's house using my better judgement. I wanted to take them to my place, so Breanna could have her room, but I didn't know what type of shit I was about to be in. My lady and baby needed to be safe, so my place was a no-go.

"Breanna, baby, come on," I spoke loudly. She was so deep into whatever movie Zuri put on that she didn't hear me. Her eyes were glued to that damn screen, so I reached back and waved the doll in her face.

"Breanna, look, it's Boo-Boo Kitty." Those big brown innocent eyes met mine. She had a huge smile on her face. Then, she moved one of the earplugs from her ear.

"Her name is Kitty, not Boo-Boo." She laughed and took the doll from my hand.

"Come on, let's get out. Give Ms. Zuri back her phone. You can watch your movie inside the house."

"Okay." She sighed, removing the second plug from her ear and handing the phone back slowly.

Zuri laughed. "It's okay, Bre, you can finish when we get inside."

We all got out the car and went to the front door. On the inside, Zuri took Breanna into the kitchen to give her a snack, while I went upstairs into the bedroom. A few minutes later, Zuri emerged by herself.

"Where's Bre?" I asked, looking to see if she was behind her.

"She's in the first bedroom, watching cartoons." Zuri walked over to me and stood in between my legs. Her gentle touch sent a warm feeling over me while she rubbed my shoulders. "Are you okay?"

"I would be lying if I said yes." My eyes drifted up to hers and all that anger resurfaced. Daddy mode was off and the savage in me had been reactivated. Somebody was gone be hurt in the morning and it damn sholl wasn't gone be me or mine. "This nigga gotta see me and gotta see me now."

"I know, baby, but you have to be careful." Zuri grabbed both of my hands and placed them on her stomach. "We can't afford to lose you and neither can Breanna. I haven't been this happy in a long time. You complete me."

That made me feel real good knowing she felt that way, but it was obvious she didn't know her man on that level. Nobody was about to take me away from the girls in my life or my unborn child. My hands remained where she placed them.

"I promise that you have nothing to worry about. When I leave here, I'm going to handle my business and I'll be back before you could miss me."

The minute I said I was leaving, Zuri's eyes instantly flooded with water. "No," she whined. "I don't want you to leave."

"This nigga tried me and I can't let it go. I'm gone show him that I ain't shit to play with. Family or no family, he gotta learn the hard way and Gucci already know how I am 'bout mine."

"What about us?" I tried to pull my hands away, but she wouldn't let them go.

All that emotional shit was making me crazy and fuckin' with my head. Whenever I stepped out and did my dirt, I pushed the ones I loved out of my head. There was no room for trial and error. Lack of attention, smothered with emotion, only meant one thing in my eyes and that was a dead man walking. There weren't many people that knew I had a daughter and it was that way for a reason.

Money always brought enemies, robberies and ransoms and I refused to put my baby in danger. Nobody needed to know what she looked like. Only God knew how many people knew her face now since I had been gone. Deja was an attention seeker and when I was away, she had my baby on Facebook. Best believe I called her ass ASAP and made her take that shit down.

"Baby, I'm coming back to all of y'all. I promise you that. Just have faith in what I'm telling you. I'm not going into anything I can't walk out of and one day, you will be able to stand on my words with ease."

Zuri finally let my hands go, so I stood up to face her. "Take Breanna to the store and get her some pajamas, clothes, underwear and whatever girly shit she need. I'm keeping her for a while."

"Okay," she replied.

"Look in that small safe under your bed and take five hundred dollars."

"Don't you think that's too much to spend? Girl clothes are cheap, baby."

"Well, do yo' thang." I pulled her close to me and covered her mouth with my lips. Our tongues slowly danced on acapella like this would be the last time we kissed, but I knew that was a lie. I mean unless the man upstairs had other plans for me. There were only two options possible, death or jail.

When I broke our kiss, Zuri was standing there with her eyes closed. Leaning in, I placed my lips on the side of her ear and licked it. "Get some sexy shit for you to sleep in, 'cause when I get back, I'm beating that pwussay down. So be ready for daddy when I get back. Or is it Zaddy?"

Zuri tried to suppress her smile, but she couldn't help herself. "I prefer the term Zaddy."

"Good. I'll see you later." Bending down, I pulled a bag from underneath the bed, removed a .380 handgun and put the bag back in its place. "I need you to do something for me."

"What?" Her eyes immediately fell to my hands.

"Take this gun and if anybody comes here and you feel threatened, shoot them. I don't give a fuck who it is. Then, call me. Not the police."

"What's going on?" There was so much nervousness in her voice.

"Nothing's going on. I just need the both of you to be safe."

"Please don't lie to me."

"I saw a white guy parked across the street and he seems a little suspicious."

I placed the gun in her hand. "Okay, I will," she replied, holding it tight in her palm.

On my way out the door, I stopped by to see my princess. "Breanna." I stood in front of the television, blocking her view. "Daddy will be back, so be good for Ms. Zuri, okay?"

"I will."

I leaned down and gave her a kiss and a hug. "I love you, baby."

"I love you too, Daddy."

Just the thought of her not being mine was killing me on the inside and that made my blood boil. It was definitely time to bounce.

"See you later, princess."

"Okay."

High tailing it out the house, I pulled my phone from my pocket and scrolled through my call log, until I came across the person I was looking for.

"Yo."

"Aye, I need a favor from you." I unlocked my car door and sat in the driver's seat. This nigga owed me his life and he was gone do whatever I told him to do. Simple as that.

***

Zuri

Brick had my nerves shot to hell. I didn't know where he was going or what he was about to do, but I knew I didn't like the sound of it. Whatever it was, I needed to know he would be okay and return to me in one piece. It was on my heart to pray for the man I loved, so I got down on both knees and folded my hands on the bed. I knew God took care of fools and babies, so I knew we both were safe. Prayer wasn't something I was good at, but I knew how to converse properly and that's what I did.

"God, I don't even know if I should be coming to you under these circumstances, but I need your help. I don't know what Brick is going to do, but you have to be a shield around him for the sake of me and his children. He's a loose cannon, but at the end of the day, he's your child and he needs your help and guidance. As selfish as I may sound, please cover him in your blood while he's causing blood to be shed amongst others. You take care of fools and we both know that he's on the top of your fool list, but I love him unconditionally. He's a piece of work, but he's a good person and I'm working on changing him and those evil ways. That's a task within itself, but I know it can be done with your help. In your name I pray, Amen."

For some odd reason, a huge weight had been lifted from my shoulders and I was able to smile. Now, it was time to take Breanna shopping, so I pulled the safe from underneath the bed and opened it. From what I could see, there were only fifties and hundreds in it. I took exactly what he told me to take and closed it back up. A lot of females I knew would take extra, but that wasn't me and I had no reason to do it. Brick would give me anything I wanted and more. All I had to do was say the word.

Standing on my feet, I grabbed my belongings and went to get Breanna from out the room. "Hey, love bug, you ready?"

She looked up and smiled. "Yes."

"Okay, come on."

"Ms. Zuri," she called out.

"You don't have to call me Ms. Zuri. That makes me feel old." I laughed.

"My daddy said that's the way to address an adult." She tilted her head to the side. "Is he wrong about that?"

"No. He's correct, but I'm telling you it's okay to just call me Zuri. Any other adult, yes, but me no."

"But why?"

Breanna was so full of questions, but it was so cute and so was she. "Because I'm your step-mama," I mumbled under my breath so she didn't hear me.

"Huh?" Her eyes never moved from my face.

"Oh, nothing." My ass play too much, but I was laughing my ass off on the inside. If she said that to her mama, that ho would probably pass out. "Come on, let's go spend your daddy's money."

"Ooh!" she screeched in excitement. "Can I get a toy?"

"Sure. I don't see why not."

"Yay!" Breanna bounced up and down.

***

It was well after six in the evening, so of course, the mall closed early on Sundays. Target was still open, so that's where we went. As we walked through the automatic doors, Breanna let go of my hand and ran to grab a buggy.

"Slow down so you don't fall." My request fell on deaf ears, because she was out of there.

Breanna met me with the buggy and a Colgate smile on her face. "Big girls don't fall."

"Oh, well excuse me, Miss Missy," I joked. "You want to get inside so I can push you?"

The way she scrunched up her face reminded me of her daddy. "Big girls don't ride in those. That's for babies."

"Well, let's go find you some clothes then."

"Don't forget the toys," she blurted out.

"How can I forget?" All I could do was laugh. That child personality was just like Brick's so there was no doubt in my mind that he wasn't her father. This girl was too much like him and that's a shame.

Breanna and I walked side by side, going through clothes in the girls section. I allowed her to show me some of the things she liked.

"Zuri."

"Yes, love bug."

"My uncle used to take me to buy clothes and to the zoo to see the animals."

"Oh really?" I asked in amusement. "I didn't know you had an uncle."

"Yeah, my mommy said he was my uncle. He did too. We used to go all the time, but I don't see him no more."

"Why is that?" I asked out of curiosity.

"I don't know." Breanna shrugged her shoulders with a bit of confusion on her face. "Sometimes he used to stay at our house and sleep with Mom."

"What you mean he sleeps with your mom?" This baby had my attention and I needed all the tea. Our conversation was better than the shit we talked about at work.

"They used to be in the room with the door closed, making noise. I think they was fighting." Breanna turned away and picked up a skirt. "Zuri, can I have this?"

"Yes." I wanted more dirt on her mammy's trifling ass. "Well, what's your uncle's name?"

"Uncle Gucci." Breanna exhaled hard and put her hands on her hips like I was getting on her itty bitty ass nerves. "You don't know my uncle Gucci?"

"As a matter I fact, I do. I've seen him around."

My mind was completely blown for the simple fact that his ho'-ass baby mama was fucking his cousin around their daughter, and parading him around like he was her real uncle. That was the foulest shit I seen all year. Brick was gone hit the fan again when he heard this.

Chapter 11

Gucci

"Damn, girl. Shit," I groaned, as I watched Mehzani ride me in the reverse cowgirl position. She was riding my shit like her ass was driving for NASCAR. Gripping her cheeks, I slowly made them bounce up and down on my wood. Her juices had my joint looking like a chocolate glazed donut stick.

Whap!

"Sss. Mmm. Hmm. Just like that," she moaned. I smacked her ass repeatedly and it jiggled like a Jell-O mold. Mehzani leaned forward, grabbing my ankles and gyrated her hips in a circular motion, giving me a clear shot of that wet pussy.

"Damn." I sighed. "I ain't gone wanna pull out you keep doing it like this."

"Bust inside of me," her voice sounded a little demonic.

Mezhani grabbed my balls and massaged them, as she continued to grind on my joystick. That shit felt so good, I almost screamed, but I had to hold it in. My toes locked up and felt like they had arthritis. This was some new shit to me, but I was enjoying it. Just as I expected an interruption. My damn phone started to ring, but I wasn't about to answer it. I was busy.

The only thing I was concerned about was busting this load. Cramps in my stomach began to surface, following behind a tingling sensation at the tip of my joint. Aggression caused me to squeeze her hips tight, penetrating her with rapid hard thrusts.

"Ahh. Ahh. Ooh. Shit."

Mehzani held on to the bed sheets for life, as her body bucked up and down. "Shit. Shit. I'm coming." I joined in with her.

My heart was beating fast as hell while I delivered steady pumps, until I started to cum inside of her. Every stroke after that was slower and slower, until I came to a complete halt. Both of my hands fell at my side and I took a deep breath.

"Whoo!" I laughed. "That's it, get up." She was still sitting on top of me.

"I ain't ready yet."

"I don't know why. We been going for like thirty minutes."

My phone started ringing again, so this time I picked up. "Yeah." I was winded like a muthafucka.

"Climb out the pussy for a few minutes, bruh. We got some urgent business to handle and it can't wait." Mel laughed on the other end of the phone.

"Who said I was in some?" I placed my finger over my lips to indicate that she needed to ride in silence.

"Nigga, can you hear yo' self-right now? Ya ass can't breathe over there." Mel was getting a kick outta that shit.

"Nigga, I was working out."

"Yeah, in some pussy."

"Fuck all that. What's going on with the business?" I tapped Mehzani on the ass. She hesitated at first, but she eventually moved and laid beside me.

"One of these niggas shady as fuck and we need to go and check his ass. I'm not gone get into it over the phone, but you catch my drift."

I sat up in the bed, swinging my legs around and planting my feet on the floor. The one thing I hated was a muthafuckin' thief and a nigga had to see me about my cash if my shit was shawt.

"You know I don't like that fuck shit. I'm 'bouta get dressed right now."

"Meet me at the spot behind the warehouses in twenty minutes."

"A'ight, I'll be there soon."

"Yeah."

As soon as I jumped up to get dressed Mehzani couldn't wait to start complaining. "Where are you going?"

"I gotta go handle some business right quick and I'll be back."

She folded her arms across her chest and pouted. "So you just gone leave me like this? That is so not fair."

"Bae, stop trippin', it's only business. Not another female, I promise." I picked up my boxers and pants from off the floor. "You heard the conversation and you know exactly who that was."

"I know, but it's too late to be out trying to conduct business. Ain't shit out this time of night, but the jack boys."

"I'll be strapped and wit' my nigga. Ain't shit gon' happen to me out here in these streets. These niggas know me and they don't want no smoke, so relax baby, okay?"

Time was ticking and I didn't have time to fuss with her right now. When I made it back home for the night, I was gone make it well worth the wait. My business was still important until I cleared it. So until then, I was still in charge. I went into the bathroom and washed my dick and balls off in the sink. I wasn't walking around smelling like pussy. After I was done getting dressed, I kissed her on the lips and headed towards the door.

Mehzani's footsteps were heavy behind me. "Baby, please don't go, it's not safe outside this time of the night. Don't you see all these niggas getting robbed and killed left and right?"

Her argument was valid and I lost a few homeboys to the streets behind the senseless killings, but that wasn't going to deter me from checking on my investment. I wasn't a flashy nigga, I stayed in my own lane and minded the business that paid me. All that other shit was irrelevant. Not once had I ever entertained social media cause that ain't shit but bait for sucka ass niggas that wanted to be seen. It was a trend to flaunt your goods and these niggas didn't believe in moving in silence. That was my motto and I lived by that shit.

A step away from the door, I stopped and turned to face my lady. "Listen, I need you to relax and go watch Tyler Perry or something until I get back. I'll be back soon and I promise, we'll finish where we left off."

"Fine, since I can't make you stay."

"This is what pays the bills, so I need to see what's up." I turned back to the door and opened it. Just as I walked out, I stuck my head back inside the door and smiled. "I love you."

"Yeah, yeah, love you too."

Ever since Mel hit me up and said it was urgent that I met up with him in twenty minutes, my head had been on a swivel ever since. Whoever it was that shorted me or tried me in any way, shape, form or fashion was about to have a real problem with me. Everyone in my camp ate damn good and I never tried feeding my niggas crumbs, so I couldn't understand why one of these bitches would cross me. It was all good, 'cause I was about to leave a nigga with his dick in the dirt and those were big factz.

When I pulled up to the warehouse, Mel was sitting on top of his car. I parked my whip behind his and stepped from the vehicle.

"What was so urgent that you had to call a nigga outside so late?" I walked up to his car and placed my foot on the bumper.

"Oh you too good to come out late?" Mel laughed, but I didn't find shit funny 'cause he emphasized the shit was urgent.

"Nah, but I was chillin' with my lady, so let's get to it so I can back to the house, 'cause she already trippin' and shit 'bout me being out late."

"Oh, this won't take long at all," he assured me.

"So, what the fuck going on with the business?" I folded my arms across my chest.

"It ain't the business. I lied." He dropped his head.

"Well, what the fuck going on?" My feet were now planted on the ground. My defensive stand was on point.

"It's about yo' girl, man."

"What about her?" Now I was confused.

Mel looked up and there was something in his eyes I never seen before. "I saw her in the dope house a few days ago."

"And, you couldn't tell me this shit over the phone?" The scowl on my face displayed my anger and I was ready to snap on his ass for making me come out for this bogus-ass shit.

"I felt like I needed to tell you in person. At least that would give you a chance to cool down, before you made it back to the house." Mel kept fidgeting with his hands.

"You straight, bruh? Why you seem so nervous?" I was good at observing behavior.

"Nah, bruh, I just don't know how to say this last part." His eyes drifted away in the opposite direction and he paused. "I saw her in there fuckin' some nigga for drugs."

"What, nigga?" The shit he just dropped on me had me ready to go back to my place and fuck her ass up before throwing her out for good. "Who the fuck was she fuckin'?"

"Fuck that ho', nigga. You know damn well you can't wife no junky."

That voice was all too familiar and when I looked to my left I was right. I nodded my head in amusement. "What the fuck you doin' here? I know you ain't come to check me about a bitch."

Brick laughed hysterically. "Fuck Deja. That ho' for everybody. You should feel the same way about yo' girl. Once a dope head, always a dope head. That ain't nobody to have a family with."

"Man, get the fuck outta here with that bullshit. I don't wanna hear shit you have to say 'cause earlier, you was talkin' real greasy."

Brick walked over and stood on the opposite side of Mel. "Well, this what I was thinking. I figured that since you falling back from the game, I should take your place. This too much territory for Mel. It needs a more," He rubbed his chin and smiled. "How should I say it? Oh yeah. A more seasoned leader."

"I ain't falling back or stepping down. So, I don't know where you getting your misleading info from." Mel was silent, so I turned my attention back to him. "You called this nigga out here?"

"Nah, bruh, I didn't. I don't know how he knew we was here." Mel's answer wasn't too convincing for me.

"I'm appalled that you don't think I'm clever enough to find you on my own. Out of all people, you should know better than that." Brick looked me up and down. "So, what the fuck you doin' then?"

"Staying off the streets. Mel will be handling business for me, so whatever you need, holla at him."

"Damn man, it's like that? You picked another nigga over your blood? That's cold." He rubbed his nose. "That's the least you could do after fuckin' my baby mama and possibly getting her knocked up." Brick shook his head and looked at Mel. "This nigga ain't got no loyalty."

"Sometimes blood ain't always thicker, but water is. You should know that." I smirked at him, because he knew exactly what I was talking about.

"Oh, it's like that?"

"You made it that way. Just be happy that I forgave you enough to put you on after you snuck home." Brick was about to say something, but my phone cut him off. I picked up. Mehzani was calling.

"What's up?"

"Are you okay?

"Yeah. Why?"

"A bad feeling came over me and I just want you to hurry up and come back home," she pleaded.

"Don't worry. I'm on my way home now." I hung up the phone. "I have to go." I glanced over at Mel. "I got some shit to handle at home. Are we done here?"

"Yeah," Mel responded.

Brick leaned up from the car. "That's it? Your final answer is no?"

I ignored that nigga and addressed Mel. Tomorrow he had a lot of explaining to do, but now wasn't the time or place and definitely not in front of this nigga. "I'll holla at you later, man. I have someone important waiting on me."

This nigga was crazy as fuck. He must've forgot about what went down some hours ago between us. Brick had some big ass monkey nuts, stepping to me like I was one of these soft-ass niggas he ran down on when he came home. I walked away thinking that he lost every marble in his goddam head if he thought I was about to let him take over my lucrative business I'd hustled hard for. He didn't know me as well as he thought.

"Aye Gucci, one more thing," Brick called out.

"What?" My feet stopped in place, but I didn't bother turning around to face the nigga, but I wish I did. All I heard were gunshots, loud and clear as I hit the ground. As I laid on my stomach gasping for air, blood poured from my mouth. In my face, all I saw were Brick's shoes as he hovered over my shaking body that had been riddled with bullets.

"Didn't I tell you to never turn your back on your enemy? It's clear that you ain't take heed to shit I taught yo' dumb ass."

Brick was right about that. He instilled that in my head over and over again, and now it was too late. I did the exact opposite.

"Fuck. You." My breathing was shallow, but I needed to get these words out before I expired. "I should've. Killed you. That night."

"Yeah, you should've, but you killed an innocent girl you stupid non-shooting muthafucka."

My eyes fluttered and my body relaxed. The last words I heard from his mouth were, *"Fuck you, nigga, we ain't blood and that bitch you wit' ain't shit either. That ho' gone be gettin' tossed up before the dirt hit ya coffin. Rest in piss and maggots, fuck nigga."* Then, I closed my eyes.

Chapter 12

Brick

After watching Gucci take his last breath, I walked away and went back over to where Mel was sitting. The look on this nigga's face was priceless. I was cracking up on the inside. His eyes were stretched to capacity and stricken with fear. Mel probably thought he was next, due to the circumstances. And the fact that I still had my strap out.

"Brick, what the fuck, man? You said all you wanted to do was talk. Why you killed the man?" his voice cracked.

"Fuck a talk. That nigga tried to kill me first." My finger was still on the trigger, just in case I had to send that nigga with his homeboy.

"What you talkin' 'bout?" he asked.

"One night, somebody sprayed my shit up and come to find out that nigga was the one who did it. So again, fuck that nigga. You got a problem with that?"

"Nah. We good, but I'm outta here before this shit gets flooded with cops and don't worry, I ain't see shit or hear shit."

"Good, 'cause you owe me your silence." Mel got in his car, then I dipped off behind the warehouse and cut through the alley to get in my car.

Gucci's face kept flashing in my mind over and over again like that shit was on repeat. While he was on the ground fighting for his life, I stood there feeling good knowing that I was responsible for issuing the death date that will be etched on his headstone. I was God in this situation.

His voice repeated itself constantly in my ears, *'Sometimes blood ain't always thicker, but that water is. You should know that.'*

When he said no, I lost it and all the old shit from our past resurfaced. And, the altercation between me and him earlier didn't make it no better. *Why did he have to bring up that old shit?* I thought we were past that. Those bones were supposed to have stayed buried. *Why did he have to open his mouth about that?* Although I wasn't

101

about to apologize for the pain I caused him and his mom in the past, he should've let sleeping dogs lie. *What more did he want from me?* That nigga provoked me and now it was his fault that I killed him.

Truth be told, I didn't kill him because he fucked Deja. She was a ho' and that's what ho's did. My problem was the fact that it involved my daughter and he wouldn't hand over his business. That nigga had a fair warning when I touched down. I told him I was taking over everything and he had the nerve to give that shit to Mel.

Gucci put this nigga on a pedestal too goddamn high and that cost him his life. I never followed him to the location. I didn't have to. Mel brought that nigga right to me. When I left Zuri and Breanna, I hit the nigga up and slid on him at his baby mama house. He was surprised I knew where she lived. That nigga was spooked when he saw me standing at the front door.

"What's up, Mel?" My killer grin made his ass stutter.

"Brick. Wha-wha-what you doing here?" He stepped onto the porch and closed the door.

"I told you that I needed to holla at 'chu."

"Yeah, I know, but how you know where my baby mama stay at?" Mel looked around to see if anyone else was lurking in the shadows.

"It's just me, so stop being so scary." I shoved my hands down in my pockets. *"I know where everybody lives. This Toya place, right? The one with your youngest kids, Melanie and Melina right?"*

"Yeah, but what that got to do with anything?" Mel's forehead had wrinkles in it.

"I do my research, but anyway, this what I need for you and before you say no, keep in mind what I know and how I get down."

"I don't like the sound of this," he said calmly.

"Do what I tell you to and it's all good. Me and Gucci beefing right now and I need you set up a meeting. He ain't gone come if he know it's me."

"A'ight. I'll do it."

***

Before going back to Zuri's place, I needed to get my mind right and take a shower, so I went home. I rolled me a fat ass blunt while I sat on my sofa listening to Tupac, "Gangsta Party." I popped a Mollie and cracked open the bottle of Hennessy that had been on my table for the past week. What was intended to be an in-and-out stop, actually turned into a two-hour solo party. During that time, Zuri called me three times and sent me a text message, asking if I was okay. Each time, I just stared at the phone and let her calls go to voicemail. It was wrong since she was worried, but I wasn't in a talking mood at the moment.

My head was fucked up and I just knew I was seeing shit. Across from me sat a female figure. She was a petite woman, but I couldn't see who she was. The longer I stared the image began to come in clearly. It was my mother.

"Look at you, son. You are so handsome, looking just like your father. Just a darker version." She smiled and crossed her legs. "I know what you did to your cousin and I'm here to tell you that you shouldn't feel bad. His mama was a dirty bitch, right along with my mama. Fuck all of them. They didn't care about us anyway. They need to suffer."

That was some freaky shit, but I loved my old girl and I wanted to see her any way I could. "Mama, I miss you so much, you just don't understand."

"I do, son. I heard you when you came to see me at the cemetery. All I wanted to do was hold you in my arms and comfort you like I did when you were younger. The same pain you feel now is how I felt when your father was murdered."

Tears filled my eyes, but I wiped them away before they could fall. "Why did you leave me? You didn't love me enough to stay?" There was never a doubt in my mind that my mother didn't love me, but I had to ask her, since she was present.

"Get that out your head. I never wanted you to feel like you were not loved. You're my only child and you meant the world to me. Always did and always will be."

"I wish you would've stayed longer. Life could be so good for you right now. We would've been happy together."

"My happiness comes from seeing you happy. Take care of the women in your life, son, and get out those streets. They don't love nobody and you know that firsthand. Look at how it did your father. I couldn't save him, but I'm going to save you. If I have to keep coming to talk to you in order for you to do the right thing, then I will. I have to go, but remember that Mama loves you."

"No, Mama, don't leave me." I sat up on the sofa, but not quick enough. Her body slowly faded away and I was now looking at an empty leather sofa.

My mind was really playing tricks on a nigga. I hadn't seen her in years, so I knew I needed to get ghost for a little while. At least, until the heat died down. I paced the floor back and forth uncontrollably, swinging my fists into midair without a target in sight. I needed to hit something, so with a closed fist, I punched the mirror hanging against the wall.

The sound of shattered glass filled my eardrums. My hands were covered in blood. I couldn't believe I killed my cousin, my blood cousin at that. Our mothers were sisters and they had the same mother and father.

I had some fucked-up ways, but I couldn't help it. I was cold-hearted and ruthless by nature. I had no choice but to play the hand I was dealt. Gucci was the same way. We were raised in the same household and we saw the same shit. Our young eyes saw shit that kids our age shouldn't have seen. We were forced into this life, because we didn't have a choice or the option to do better.

After my mother passed away, I was constantly going in and out of juvenile hall. I had also developed this hate for females, but when I met Déjà she changed all of that. She loved me for the villain that I was and never judged me. She was the only female alive at that time who had the ability to change me and make me a better person. In my mind I felt that without her I would always disrespect women, but that was false as fuck. She ended up being the one that brought out the worst in me.

When Deja left me for dead in the pen, I made a promise to the devil that I would kill her when I got out. The night after the club when we were in my hotel room, I thought about choking her to death in her sleep, but I couldn't pull myself to do it. After all, that dirty bitch was still the mother of my child, so I gave her a pass.

Due to a twisted chain of events, right in the middle of me escaping something that could've landed me in prison with an L, or dead, I was blessed to run into an angel at that time of the night. She could've easily blew the whistle on me that night, but she aided me to safety and patched me up. I had a real woman on my arm and would never mistreat her the way I did these ho's. Zuri was a true queen and she deserved everything I could get my hands on. I owed that woman my life.

Now, here I was, standing in my living room with blood on my hands, literally and figuratively. I didn't know what was coming my way, but I knew prison wasn't an option. I meant exactly what I said when I came home. *I would rather be carried by six, instead of judged by twelve.* I refused to grace the prison system with my presence again and I meant that shit.

Chapter 13

Zuri

On edge, I sat on my dining room floor, crying my eyes out hysterically at five in the morning. Every call and text that I placed to Brick went unanswered. My heart was hurting so bad and I was stressed the fuck out to the point I couldn't sleep. I didn't know if he was dead or alive and that didn't sit well with my spirit. It hurt more when Breanna asked me about his whereabouts. My heart couldn't take another loss. It was bad enough that I lost my brother, so to lose the father of my child is something I couldn't deal with.

She wanted to know if he would be back to tuck her in for bed, but I couldn't pull myself to tell her no. To keep her occupied, we had root beer floats while watching the *Incredibles*. Around nine o' clock, I ran her a bubble bath and let her play with the toys we picked up. That lasted close to an hour. By the time I read her a bedtime story, Breanna was knocked out and snoring. She was loud for a little girl.

The sudden noise from the front door snatched my attention and increased the speed of my heart. A huge lump formed in my throat, as I waited for him to come inside. Brick pushed the door open and crossed the threshold, securing the locks behind him. Unable to contain my emotions, I rushed in his direction, throwing my arms around his neck.

"Baby, I was so worried about you. I couldn't sleep at all." Tears cascaded down my face.

Brick held me tight in his muscular arms. "I'm sorry I had you worried, but I couldn't answer my phone."

Upon our release, I took a step back to examine him. The last time he was involved in some mess, he ended up with a flesh wound from being shot. My hands trembled as I raised his shirt checking for any wounds. He grabbed my hands.

"Baby, relax. I'm okay." His eyes were low, yet filled with so much compassion. Brick wiped my tears away with his fingers.

"I thought I was never going to see you again. That you would never see our baby and I would have to raise our child alone."

He held my face gently with both hands. "You have nothing to worry about. I'm not going anywhere and I promise you that. It's gone take a muthafuckin' army to take me out."

Brick leaned down and kissed me softly. His touch made me moist on contact. The smell of marijuana was on his breath, but I didn't mind at all. I was just happy to have my man home and in one piece. My baby lifted me in his arms and carried me up the steps.

"How was Bre?" He peeked in the room, as we walked by.

"She was good, but when it was time for bed, she wanted you to tuck her in."

"Since I've been home, I make it my business to tuck her in as much as possible."

"That's so sweet, baby. You're a great father."

When we made it to my bedroom, he closed the door and locked it before putting me down. He looked at me with so much hunger in his eyes, causing my cat to thump to a sexual beat. I returned the same glance.

"Take them clothes off and get up in that bed." He didn't have to tell me twice. I rushed over and stripped like I was racing against the clock.

Brick walked over to the nightstand, took out a small box and placed it underneath the pillow. Crawling onto the bed, I laid on my back and waited anxiously for him to make love to me. He hopped in the bed and kneeled between my legs.

"Spread them legs wide open and keep 'em just like that." I loved when he talked to me all aggressive and shit. He reminded me of Jeezy.

As I stretched my legs open, I placed my hand on my flower and spread my petals open, so he could see my cotton candy pink center. Brick licked his lips and glared down at my kitty in excitement. Slowly, I rubbed my pearl.

"Ahh." I rocked my hips from side to side, getting myself aroused.

Brick placed his head between my thighs. The sudden rapid flick of his tongue against my center sent an electric jolt up my spine. His lips French kissed my mine and I melted in ecstasy. He slurped and sucked on my pearl.

"Ss. Ooh. Yes, baby." My eyes were clenched tight, while I rubbed the top of his head. My legs kept trying to lock up on me, so the battle was definitely real. Brick had a fat hurricane tongue and it was hard to stay in one spot.

"Let me eat this muthafucka." Brick spit on sally cat and slurped on her hard. I felt his finger penetrate me. The rapid movement was enough to make me cum quickly. My insides were screaming to dish out a creamy shower.

"Shit. Shit. Brick. Fuck."

"Feel good, don't it?"

"Yes. Yes. I want the dick now," I moaned loudly, pulling him closer to me.

"I told you I'll be back." Brick rubbed the tip of his head up and down my slit, teasing me on purpose. His ass knew I was feenin' and he wanted to play.

"I know. Put it in." I was trying to get close enough to put it in myself.

"Next time I say I'm coming back, take my word for it." He grinned.

"Okay, I will. Now stop playing."

Brick finally pushed the head in and I was relieved when I felt his dick fill me up. My vagina muscles gripped him tight while massaging his dick, as he thrusted in and out of my gushy nookie.

"Ahh. Ss. Oh my God." Damn, he knew what to do to my body. I held my knees so I could feel every inch of my magic stick.

"Ooh, yeah. This feel like new pussy every time I get in it," he moaned.

I kept my eyes closed, as I bit down on my lip. "Mm. Mm. Mm." Brick sunk deeper and increased his pace, and the sound of our skin slapping filled my ears. That drove me crazy. "Ooh. Yes. Beat this pussy. Shit." My breathing was all out of whack.

"What my pussy 'bout to do?" Brick wanted to ask questions, but I was damn near speechless. He pushed his weight down on me and dug deeper. "What my pussy 'bout to do?"

The aggression in his voice made me find the strength to respond. "It's about to come, Zaddy."

"Hell yeah," he grunted. "Make that fat pussy come on yo' dick."

Rough sex with Brick always made me feel like I was out of shape. My breathing was heavy like I was in the middle of doing the five-mile run. I was flexible, but that didn't mean shit when he was in it because that shit still hurt. He pushed my legs back further, spit on my vagina and slapped it with his hand.

"Talk dirty or I ain't lettin' you go." The head of his dick kissed my uterus and I hollered his name like I was singing in the choir at the church.

"Briiiicckk!"

"Oh, you can't take it, huh?"

"Ooh, you deep in this pussy. I can feel it in my stomach." That was the truth too. My eyes felt hot and I could feel tears building up. Both of my hands were planted firmly on his chest in an effort of getting him to pull a few inches out, so I could breathe. Apparently, it worked, because he pulled it all the way out and dropped my legs.

"Come on and get on top."

Brick laid on his back, so I could straddle him. I slid down on him slowly and rocked back and forth. "Oh yeah, I'm bouta lay back, enjoy this ride and muthafuckin' view."

It was my time to shine. I grinded hard in a circular motion, while rubbing my clit at the same time. Brick's moans were so damn erotic since he had this hard-ass demeanor. He smacked my ass hard and I could feel it jiggle.

"Bounce on it. I wanna see that dick go in and out that pretty pussy."

Immediately, I got on my feet and did what Zaddy wanted. "Ooh, shit. She a rider. Keep it right there." Bricked squeezed both of my cheeks and met my thrusts.

"Don't you move. Damn. Don't you move." His movements rocked the bed, as he thrusted his hips up and down.

"Ooh. Baby," I panted. Dropping my head to the side caused my leg to move. "Dammit, Zaddy." He was killing me.

Whap!

That was the sound of him smacking the brown off my ass. "I told you not to move."

"Okay. Okay."

"Ride it sideways," he demanded.

Straddling one of his legs, I leaned forward and grabbed his ankle. While grinding on it, I felt heavy vibrations against my bootyhole. At first I jumped because it caught me off guard, but I knew it was the new bullet he bought.

"Be still."

Brick spread my juices from my pussy to my asshole before penetrating it with the bullet. This was the first time we used any toys and I think I liked it already. He pushed it in and out slowly. The intense pressure of the vibrations and penetration in both holes made me cum again, but much harder in under five minutes.

"Ahh! I'm cummin." My body shook like I was having a seizure. In all my years of being sexually active, I had never felt an orgasm that was so intense.

Brick sat up and pushed me forward. "Face down and arch that back."

He just didn't know that I was through dealing and I was praying he made his nut snappy. Shit, I was ready to go to sleep now. I buried my head in the pillow and arched my back. Brick dove right it in and pounded my nookie from behind. Occasional slaps followed. The pillow came in handy, because my girl was sore and the friction alone was about to make me cry real tears. I was able to maintain and wear my big girl panties until I heard his grunts intensify.

"Ooh, shit. I'm cummin'." His pelvis slapped against my ass hard.

"Fuuck!" I screamed.

"Where you want me to nut at?"

I turned my head to the side so he could hear me loud and clear. "Inside of me."

Hell, I was already pregnant, so it didn't matter where he put it. I just wanted him to stop.

"Whoo! Whoo!" Brick started to slow down and damn, was I relieved.

Smack!

I was convinced he liked the sound of his hand against my ass.

"Damn, I think I'm sprung." He laughed and pulled his limp soldier out of hiding. My body instantly hit the mattress. Brick collapsed right after me in the spot he was in and looked over at me.

"If I ever catch you cheating or suspect it, I'm killing you with no hesitation and I put that on my mama."

Brick was as jealous as they came and he could be very irrational. I experienced that first quarter and we wasn't together when he ran down on me and Jason.

"I can say the same thing." I smiled.

"Nah, I ain't gone cheat. I don't have a reason to. I have all I need right here." He rubbed my chin with his thumb.

"So do I," I replied.

"Good answer." He laid there, looking in my eyes for a few seconds. "You not going to work tomorrow."

"I don't know."

"No, I'm telling you that you not going. It's six in the morning so call out. I'll pay you for the day."

"Okay. I'll call them."

Absences weren't my thing, but I did anticipate staying home, since I didn't get any sleep. My ass was tired, so I cuddled underneath Brick and closed my eyes.

"Oh, remind me to tell you something in the morning." I yawned.

"Why you can't tell me now?"

"I'm sleepy, baby. Can I get some rest first, please?"

"Yes," he agreed.

"Okay, goodnight."

Whenever I got up, I was going to fill him in on everything Breanna told me about Deja and Gucci. I knew by telling him, it was going to cause more problems, but he had every right to know what was going on around his daughter. As a mother, I couldn't understand Deja's trifling behavior. It was bad enough she was fucking his first cousin, but to blatantly do it in front of their daughter was totally disrespectful and that's why I felt no remorse when he beat her ass. She deserved that shit. Gucci was no better than her and he deserved whatever Brick had planned for him.

Chapter 14

Mehzani

Daylight welcomed in the next day and I had been up all night, waiting on Gucci to come home. He wasn't answering his phone or responding to any of my text messages. I was livid and worried at the same time, but of course, the mad outweighed the worry. All I kept thinking about was if he was someplace having sex with Deja. I didn't understand it, because he made a promise that he would never hurt me again.

Why would he tell me all of those things and turn around and re-enact the very thing that almost tore us apart? I really thought I was special in his eyes and my days of heartache were long gone. Gucci promised not to hurt me the way everyone else did. I confided in him with my struggles, family issues and my drug urges.

Here I was, once again sulking in my own tears, without a shoulder to cry on. Maybe he couldn't see past my old ways and still saw me as the young girl on flakka. However, that was a thing of the past, because I hadn't used drugs since we became a couple. That was my promise to him and I was going to keep it. All I could do was curl up into a ball and cry. I was hugging the pillow and staring at his picture, hoping he would come home soon. Maybe this was karma finding a way to get back at me. The original plan wasn't for me to fall in love with him, but now that had changed.

The loud banging on the door caused my heart to drop to the floor. It sounded like a police knock. The type they give before kicking the door off the hinges. I knew he sold drugs, but I didn't know how deep he was in the game. Too afraid to get up, I sat there biting my nails until I heard my name. That alone made me run to the door to see who it was. When I opened it, standing in front of me was Melvin and he didn't look too good.

He barged in without saying a single word to me and that alone had me frightened. "Gucci got shot last night."

Those words were a punch to the stomach. My legs moved as fast as they could so I could get next to the sofa. It was a good idea, but halfway there, I lost all balance and fell onto the floor. My heart was beating like a drum and I couldn't get my words together. "What?"

"He's in the hospital and I don't think he's going to pull through. So, hurry up and get dressed, just in case he takes a turn for the worst."

Without another word, I ran into the bedroom and put on some sweatpants and a t-shirt. Then, we were out the door, in route to see my baby. Melvin drove at a high rate of speed, but it still took us about twenty-five minutes to get there because we stayed out west. The minute the car hit the parking lot, I jumped out and ran towards the entrance. Gucci needed me in order to make it and I needed to see his face.

I hated hospitals, they reminded me of death. The smell alone killed me. It was like I could feel the Grim Reaper hovering over my back. I walked briskly behind Melvin, as he led the way. He had to really love Gucci, because he had been crying from the time we got in the car, until we arrived.

Melvin walked into the room and I stopped dead in my tracks. I had to brace myself for what I was about see, so I took a deep breath before I walked in. My steps were heavy, but slow, as if I was walking through quicksand. The room was cold and it felt like death was lingering in the air. My hands were shaking and my heart was beating rapidly.

Gucci was laying in the bed, completely incapacitated. There were tubes all over his body going in every direction. It hurt to see the man I wanted and needed stare death in the eyes. The thought of him leaving me behind pierced my heart. I was in pain and the guilt was sinking in.

Not too long ago, my selfish ass was straddled across his bed crying, thinking he was out here cheating and all this time he was somewhere fighting for his life. I found the strength to step closer to the bed and touch his hand. My man was lukewarm to the touch and it frightened me. Tears began to fall, making tiny splashes on the bed. I was crying because of his pain, my pain, our pain. If he died I might as well be dead too, because I couldn't fathom living without him and I wasn't willing to try it either. I needed him like a crack head needed a fix. Like a cancer patient needed chemo. He was my rehab and I knew I couldn't make it without him. When I looked up, Melvin was looking in my direction.

"You straight?"

"No. I feel horrible. I thought he was out cheating on me last night and this is what was happening."

"He loves you. He would never jeopardize losing you. He talks about you all the time."

Obviously, he didn't know his boy that well, since he was recently caught cheating. I needed to look at him, so I could see where he was shot at. My nosey ass lifted the soft blanket he was snuggled up under and then his gown and I damn near screamed.

"Is that a—" I paused mid-sentence.

"Shit bag," Melvin completed my sentence and I took off running into the bathroom. I threw up all the food I consumed the day before. That was my first time in life ever seeing a colostomy bag and my actions just proved that. Melvin stood at the door, calm as can be.

"You good?" he asked sincerely.

"I can't see him like this."

"Come on, I'll take you home."

With my head hanging over the toilet in deep thought, I shook my head. "No I can't leave him."

"Are you sure?"

"Yes."

Melvin stepped away from the door without another word. In my heart I could honestly say that he was very loyal to Gucci. I had never seen a bond so strong, especially when money was involved. Those dead presidents were always the root of all evil, which made me feel the shooting had something to do with his drug business. After I cleaned myself up and stepped from the bathroom, Melvin had his head down and I could tell that he was hurting as much as I was, if not more, so I decided to make small talk.

"Are you okay?" I asked, as I stood beside the chair he was sitting in.

117

"Only if he pulls through." He sighed.

"You're really close, I see."

"He's like a brother to me, a blood brother." Melvin looked up and I could see the sincerity, along with the pain in his eyes. He seemed to be broken up about it. "My mom passed away when I was fourteen. Gucci and his mom looked out for me when my own family wouldn't. Our brotherhood means the world to me and I don't know what I would do without him. I owe him my life and whoever did this gone have to see me. I'm burying any and everybody that had something to do with this. I don't give a fuck who it is. He has my loyalty until I take my last breath."

We were two people with different purposes that shared one connection and we loved Gucci to death. I leaned down and gave him a hug.

"We're going to get through this together," I promised.

Our embrace was cut short by a long, dragged-out constant beeping noise. I watched enough movies to know that was a flat line, due to the stopping of the heart rate. The piercing sound penetrated my ears and a loud scream escaped my mouth. My legs felt like wet noodles beneath me and I could no longer carry my own weight. I could feel my body dropping to the floor in slow motion. Then, I could feel a set of strong hands grab me and break my fall. Melvin called out for help and the nurses came running.

"Code blue," one of the nurses shouted.

Everything was happening so fast and I couldn't contain my emotions. "Noo," I screamed. "Please don't leave me."

The nurse looked at Melvin and pointed towards the door. "Sir, please take her out in the hallway." He grabbed my arms, but I was determined to stay by Gucci's side.

"Save him please. I can't live without him."

He was still flat lining when they closed the door behind us. I knew it was over, but I didn't want to accept that fact. A piece of me died at that very moment. I had just witnessed the love of my life's heartbeat stop and take his last breath. My life was over!

***

Brick

The sound of laughter made me stir in my sleep, interrupting a very nasty pornographic scene in my dream. Slowly blinking, a pair of tiny fingers were holding my eyelids, followed by more laughter.

"Wake up, Daddy," Breanna screeched, bouncing up and down on the bed.

"Ahhh," I grunted, while stretching my arms.

"That noise sounds familiar." Zuri giggled.

"I bet it do. That's how you sounded this morning, but high-pitched." Breanna's head swiveled in both directions with her nosey ass. "Good morning, princess."

"It's not morning anymore." The way she frowned made me laugh.

"Oh shit, what time is it?" Instantly panicking, I sat up and looked for my phone.

"Relax, baby, it's only one thirty," Zuri replied. "I know you have a meeting at three. That's why we are waking you up."

It was strange she knew that, because I never mentioned it. "How you know?"

"Coop was blowing up your phone, so I answered it because I figured it was important. He told me not to wake you up at that time, but to make sure you got up in time for the meeting."

Breanna sat there in silence, playing with her doll.

"Oh, good. I thought I was late." Satisfied it was still early, I laid back down and took the doll from her hands. "You show this doll more attention than me."

"I'm her mommy."

"You ain't having no babies."

"Really, Brick?" Zuri cut her eyes at me. "She's only six."

"I don't care about that. She needs to know that I ain't nobody's granddaddy."

Zuri shook her head. "You crazy for real."

"You better know that shit." I got up and sat on the edge of the bed. "Did you call in today?"

"Yeah, but they still have me on leave."

"Ooh, Daddy, she said yeah." Bre covered her mouth and her eyes were stretched wide as a baseball.

Since my daughter was in our presence, I had to correct her. "Yeah, or you meant to say yes?"

Zuri appeared confused as she gave me the side eye with her lip tooted up. "What?"

"Yeah isn't the proper term. I'm teaching Bre the correct way to speak, so I don't need to contradict myself."

"Okay," she paused for a split second. "Yes, I did call in today."

Both of my hands were positioned behind my head, resting comfortably. "I'll pay you for the day and for keeping Bre while I go to the meeting."

"You don't have to pay me for that." Zuri always made it her business to decline any monetary offers from me, but being the man I am, I wasn't hearing that shit.

"I know I don't have to, but I'm doing it since you called out for me."

"Okay, I won't argue with that."

"You won't win." I winked at her. "Take Bre to watch TV and come back. I need to talk to you."

"Yeah, I bet." Zuri got up from the bed. "Come on, love bug, let's go."

"Bye, Daddy." She crawled in Zuri's direction.

"No kiss before you leave? And, I can't get a pet name?" I shook my head. "Y'all gettin' real close."

"Cut it out. I call you Zaddy."

"Facts."

Breanna came back and gave me a kiss on my lips.

"I love you, princess."

"I love you too, Daddy."

"Aww, that's so sweet." Zuri picked Breanna up, placing her on her hip.

"Zuri?" She played with one of her plaits.

"That's Ms. Zuri," I corrected Bre.

"I told her not to call me that." She swatted me away like I was some damn fly. "Yes."

"Do you love my daddy too?"

Zuri simply smiled and replied. "Yes, I do."

The minute the coast was clear, I hopped out the bed and scurried my naked ass into the bathroom. My dick and balls was slanging left and right. Her ass must've forgot that I didn't have on any clothes when we went to bed earlier that morning. I stood over the toilet draining the python with my head held back. That was a huge relief. It felt like I had been holding that shit in all day. There was a light tap on the door before I heard it open, but I didn't say anything.

"Pissing with no hands, huh?" Zuri asked.

The last drop of piss hit the water, so I brought my head forward then flushed the toilet. When I turned around, Zuri was just standing there looking at me like I was her next meal.

"Close your mouth." It was obvious sex was on her mind, so I grabbed my dick and shook it. "When you packin' all this steel you don't need to hold it. I got my big nigga trained."

"Yeah, I see."

"Why you looking at me like that? You want some don't it?" We locked eyes and I licked my lips.

"Ahem." She cleared her throat. "I would love to, but that's not why I came in here."

The seriousness in her eyes snatched my attention and released my grip on my piece. "What happened?"

Zuri took a deep breath and scratched her head. "I don't really know how to say this."

She was never the type to be lost for words and that made me a little concerned. "It don't matter, just say it."

"Last night, Breanna told me that Gucci used to spend the night and they would have the door closed."

If I was drunk or high, that shit would've blew it fa 'sho. "What?"

"She said they used to be fighting, but you know what that really means?"

My jaw was clinched tight in anger. "Yeah, they was fuckin' wit' my daughter in there. I should go over there and beat that bitch ass again."

That nigga was lucky he was dead already. On my mama, if he wasn't, I would've busted his ass in broad daylight wherever I caught him at. I didn't give a fuck at that moment. It was time for a drink, so I went to wash my hands.

"Baby," Zuri's voice was low when she called out to me. "You not going back over there, are you?"

I was so goddamn mad I couldn't say shit. "Brick, answer me," she repeated, but all I could do was stand there and look at her. "Please don't go back over there. The damage is already done and I'm sure you did major damage to her already. Just let it go."

She walked up to me and placed her hand on my chest. "I love you and the three of us need you. Don't throw it away. The only thing that matters is that you are here and back in Breanna's life."

A woman like Zuri was what I needed. Someone to calm down the inner beast within me. She was my calm in the midst of a storm, and my peace after dealing with these fuck niggas in the streets.

"I love you too and I won't go over there."

She bent her head slightly to the side. "You promise?"

"I promise."

That was going to be a hard promise to keep on Deja's behalf, but on the strength of Zuri, I would do my best. "I promise."

"Thank you." Zuri ran her hand down my chest, stopping at my abs. "I couldn't fathom losing all of this."

Just her touch alone made my shit stand at attention. I was supposed to be getting ready for my meeting early, but I couldn't resist the temptation. Instead of getting in the shower, I scooped her up in my arms and carried her into the bedroom. I wasn't leaving the house with blue balls, so a quickie was about to go down.

Chapter 15

Kyra

As I pulled into the driveway of my aunt's house, the faint sound of my cellphone could be heard ringing through the IMO app. Quickly, I put the car in park to locate it. My purse was in the front seat so I fished around in it, but came up empty-handed. It continued a few more times before it stopped. Seconds later, it started right back up.

My common sense kicked in and I turned off the radio to see if I could hear exactly where it was coming from. The sound was coming from behind me, so I leaned back and checked the floor. Lo and behold, it had slid underneath the seat. When I finally grabbed it and checked the screen, I realized it was a call I had been waiting on. There was so much excitement in my voice when I picked up, although I tried to hide it.

"Hello."

"Yeah." Daman didn't seem to be happy about hearing my voice, but he called me though.

"Well, don't sound so dry." He couldn't see me rolling my eyes through the audio call. "You could try to be happy to hear my voice."

"Now, why in the fuck would I be happy to hear from you?" Daman snapped.

"Why wouldn't you be?" I asked.

"Why would you tell her about me and you? That was something that was supposed to remain hidden. Now she mad and not answering any of my calls because of that shit you pulled."

"We had an argument and it slipped. It was never intentional. She provoked me and before I knew it I just blurted it out."

"I don't believe that, but okay. If you said that's what happened then it is what it is."

"Here it goes." I sucked my teeth hard to make sure he heard it. "No matter what happens, Kyra's word don't count for shit and Zuri can never do any wrong."

"Kyra," he sighed. "You said there was something going on with Zuri, so what is it?"

"See, and that's exactly what I'm talking about." I put the phone on speaker, because I was ready to curse his ass out too, but not before I burst his bubble.

"You know what," I dragged the hell out of the word *what* just because. "You steady trying to defend Zuri, when she out here living her best ho' life."

"What the fuck you talkin' 'bout?" The hostility in his voice appeared fast.

"You a fool if you believe she stopped answering her phone because of me. Zuri been fucking this dude name Brick since he got out the feds not too long ago."

"How you know that?" he asked.

"I was with her when they met in the club. Then afterwards, she went home with him all drunk and shit. I tried to get her to go home, but I guess she just wanted some dick."

"Nah, she wouldn't do no shit like that." His ass was in denial.

"If you say so." I sucked my teeth. Daman's ass was really pissing me off. "I was there so I would know and I'm not just saying that because we not friends anymore."

"The nigga name Brick, huh? What's his real name?" he asked.

"It's Brandon, but I don't know his last name. His cousin name Gucci. He be in the city trappin' sometimes."

"A'ight. Good lookin' out. I'll get up with you later. I got some shit to do right now."

"Oh, so that's it?"

"Chill out, man. My cellie just came back in from work and he wanna shower. I'll call you back."

"Yeah, okay."

"You—"

My finger found the end button quick and whatever he was about to say went unheard. I didn't have time to listen to that bullshit he was about to kick, so I snatched my shit up and got out the car. On the porch, Kamari was sitting on the step, talking to one of his friends.

"What's up Kyra?" Kamari looked over his shoulder.

"You ready to go?"

"Yeah. I'm coming." Kamari stood up and dapped his homeboy. "I'll get at 'chu later, man, and make sure you holla at dude for me."

"I'm on it. I'm 'bout to meet up with him in a few anyway. I'll tell you what he said."

"A'ight, cool."

As soon as his boy walked off, Kamari got up and we went inside the house.

"Where is Auntie Anne?"

"She went to the store," he replied.

"Oh, okay. Well get your stuff so we can go."

"A'ight."

Kamari went to the back while I sat down on the couch. Every time I stepped foot in that house, it dredged up old memories of the time I had to live here and hide my pregnancy from my friends. Kamari was the spitting image of his daddy and there was no denying that. I wondered how my life would be right now had I not given him up. Just looking at him made me regret my past and the fact that I didn't fight for what I wanted. Him.

***

Brick

Five minutes to three, I pulled up to my house. Before I did my bid, I purchased it when it went into foreclosure for the sole purpose of conducting business out of it. While I was away, Coop came through and checked on it for me. He always conducted his business out of it as well, but that was all good because he did me a justice.

Four cars were in the driveway, but one was missing. For his sake, Tone better be carpooling with someone and not running late. Everyone had ample time to get there, so I didn't want to hear any excuses. That shit was unacceptable and he knew better. The block was quiet with the exception of a few kids riding past on their bikes. As always, my phone went to vibrating in my pocket, but the trash on the side of the road had my attention.

"These kids gone make me kick they lil' asses for littering on my damn property," I ranted.

Slowly, I pulled out my phone and screened the call. My first thought was to send her ass to voicemail, but I quickly changed my mind.

"Yo."

"Hey, stranger. What's going on with you?" Jessica asked in a cheery voice.

"Nothing much. About to walk into a meeting."

"Ohh." She sighed. "I guess I should call back then?"

"Not if you can spit your purpose before it starts in the next five minutes."

"Oh. I was just trying to see if you if you was ready for me? Because, I'm definitely ready for some more dick."

I unlocked the front door with my key and walked inside. "Just like that, huh?" The living room was empty as it should be. That meant everyone was in place and awaiting my arrival.

"Yess," She hissed. "My pussy so hot and moist thinking about you right now."

All of that sounded good and knowing her, she was probably playing in her pussy, but I wasn't trying to find out. I had business to handle. "Aye, I gotta go. I'll hit you up later."

Jessica sucked her teeth. "Yeah."

I disconnected the call before I walked through the door that led into the garage. That area was closed off and used for meeting purposes only. The moment I stepped in and closed the door, all of the chatter stopped abruptly. Coop was sitting with his hands folded underneath his chin. He looked up and we slapped hands.

"What's good, bruh?" he asked.

"Tired as fuck," I replied.

"Yeah, I know. Ya lady told me." Coop sat up straight. "Oh yeah, I handled what we talked about. They'll be here after the meeting."

"Good looking out."

As I stepped up to my table, I noticed Chris was slumped in his seat. I slammed my keys down hard on the table intentionally to get his attention.

"Sit up straight when I come in this muthafucka. Fuck wrong wit' 'chu?" Chris jumped up and sat at attention. "I don't know what the fuck going on in y'all heads, but y'all betta get in check and recognize who run shit around here."

"My bad. I got a hangover and I was just resting my eyes since you was late."

That nigga must've bumped his head. My top lip curled and my eyes lowered to his. "Who the fuck was late?"

"Um. N-nobody," he stuttered.

"When I walk in, you sit up straight. I don't give a fuck if I was late."

"A'ight, my bad."

"That's what the fuck I thought." I pulled my chair out and sat down. "Let's get one thing muthafuckin' straight. I'm never late. I don't give a fuck what the clock says."

Tone, Skeet and Wayne sat there in silence. Their eyes never left mine. I had their undivided attention and that's what the fuck I needed.

"Did everybody turn in their money?" I leaned back in my seat and acknowledged them all one by one. They all replied with a head nod. I looked over at Coop.

"How much did you collect?"

"Two hundred seventy-five bands."

It was beneath my goal, so I needed to see who was lacking. "So that means we twenty-five bands short from the weekly quota. "Skeet, how much did you clear off the block?"

"Ninety bands," he said with confidence.

"That's more than you were supposed to do, but I'll come back to you on that." I turned my attention to the sick one. "Mr. Hangover, what 'chu had?" I was ready for him to say he was short, since he always ready for the turn up.

"Seventy-five," Chris replied coolly.

"Wayne." I nodded in his direction.

"Seventy-five," Wayne answered with ease.

"Tone." The look in his eyes and his hesitation told me everything I needed to know before he opened his mouth.

"Thirty-five." His response was very low. It wasn't like I couldn't count and didn't know he was the short one in the group.

"Speak up for the ones in the back that can't hear you." It may have appeared as a joke to some, but I was dead-ass serious.

"I only did thirty-five. It was hard for me to move that shit fast." He sunk down in his seat.

"So, you are the weakest link of the group." Pushing my seat back, I stood up and rubbed my hands together. "So, that means Skeet sold some of your work while you was out doing whatever?"

"He had more clientele than I did, so I gave it to him. I mean, it still got sold."

My fist crashed against the table and shook it, as I yelled, "Yeah muthafucka, but you ain't sell shit. What the fuck I'm paying you for?"

Tone sat there all bug eyed and shit like he didn't have a clue what was going on.

"I don't need you here takin' up space and lookin' for a free muthafuckin' ride. If these niggas can get out and get that money, you can too. I need hungry niggas."

"Come on, Brick, don't do me like that. I need this man. This how I eat." Tone tried pleading his case, but I wasn't trying to hear that shit.

"Nigga, this how I muthafuckin' eat and feed my family. You think those muthafuckin' Cubans wanna hear we can't get rid of this fuckin' product? Fuck, no. I done told y'all this a grown man's game and if you ain't ready, stay on the muthafuckin' porch."

"Oh, he been the porch alright," Coop spoke up. "I slid up on the nigga the other night to see how the shit was moving and he was entertaining some crackhead ho'."

"I hope that ho' wasn't smoking my shit on the house or in exchange for some cracked-out, coked-up, ran-through pussy." Tone was two seconds from getting his ass flipped.

"Come on, Coop, you was there. You saw what was going on." He sat up in his seat. "Brick, I ain't give her shit on the house. I swear."

I wasn't convinced.

"Nigga, she looked mighty fuckin' comfortable while I was standing there." Coop stood up. "Brick, the nigga seemed high to me. He said he had been drinking, but I don't buy that shit."

"G-Shit?" Coop's word was gold, so anything he said held up at any given time.

"G-Shit," Coop replied.

We stood there with our arms folded. Everybody else was just taking it all in. "What you think we should do 'bout this nigga?" I asked Coop.

"I say we get rid of the nigga. It's too many young niggas out here trying to chase that bag."

"Yeah, I think that's best for all of us. I mean, if Skeet selling his work, then I don't need him. He can take over his clientele." We spoke as if he wasn't in the room. Then, I turned my attention to Skeet. "What you think 'bout that youngin'?"

My protégé looked at me and replied, "You know I'm down for whatever and if you need me to double up, then I'm up for the task."

"See, Tone, that's what I need right there. You a waste and your presence is pointless." That nigga was baked chicken. I was all about my cash flow and I didn't have time to babysit no grown-ass man.

"Come on, Brick, give me another chance. I just need a little more time to get it done. Please," Tone begged.

"You got seventy-two hours to sell twenty-five grand in product. If you can't do that, then you out of here and that's a promise."

"Okay," Tone agreed, but I knew he couldn't do it and he knew it too. However, that would make his departure easier. That would leave him responsible for his own demise.

"You know damn well you can't push that shit, man. Just quit while you ahead. This nigga just trying to buy time." Coop was disgusted and wasn't too keen on second chances to keep from shedding blood. Me, on the other hand, I was willing to let him hang himself and when the time came, I would kick the chair from beneath his feet.

Skeet rubbed his hands together. "Well, I got a homeboy, and he solid as fuck. He interested in the position. I can take him under my wing and show him the ropes."

"You vouching for that nigga?" I tested.

"Yeah." He looked me in the eyes when he spoke and I respected him for that. Eye contact was important to weed out a muthafucka who bullshittin' you. In all my years of living, niggas with ill intentions and smoke blowers could never look you dead in the face and lie. All but Gucci. That nigga looked me in the face and lied on the regular.

"I'm willing to sit down with him, but if he fuck up, I'm holding you responsible."

"He solid and he ain't gone fuck up."

"So is ice, but when that heat get ahold to it, that shit melts." I nodded my head in his direction. "You catch my drift?"

"I do, but this my nigga and I wouldn't bring him to you if he was a snitch."

"A'ight, set up a meeting for us to meet."

"Okay."

Coop and I took our seats so I could bring the meeting to a close. "So, in the next few days the shipment will be here and I need everyone to hit the ground running. Get your people in order and make sure they're on standby with that money. Every muthafucka on the roster should be ready to re-up by the time it get here."

Chris raised his hand and with a head nod, I acknowledged him so he could speak. "I think we gone have a problem with one of Legend's boys. One of his people's was at my dealer's place of business, trying to move in on our territory by low balling."

"Who is this nigga?" That had me curious, because it sounded like somebody was trying to step on my toes and get a reaction out of me.

"Some dude name Raheem. Ion know the nigga, but he one of them country bamas that Legend brought down with him." Chris leaned forward and folded his hands in front of him.

Any muthafucka that thought he was about to move in on what I was building had another thing coming. I bit down on my lip and nodded my head. "See, that ain't about to happen and next time you see that nigga tell him I want to meet up with him. He gone have two options and both of 'em non-negotiable."

"Bruh, we don't need a war right now. We trying to expand and killing off too many muthafuckas too risky." Coop disagreed, but I didn't care because if push came to shove, we was bussing them guns no matter what the outcome was.

"Yeah, I know that, but what the fuck you think we supposed to do if he try some shit?" I sighed and looked him in the eyes. "I get what you saying and that's why we gone have a sit-down first. If that shit don't work, then you know what has to happen."

"Agreed." Coop's phone went off and he looked down at it. It had to be a text, because he started typing. "They here, so gone and dismiss them." Then, he got up and left the room.

"The meeting is over, so y'all free to go." Just when I thought shit was about to be smooth sailing, I get hit some more shit. They all stood up.

"Yo, Brick." Chris approached me and stopped a foot away from me. "Raheem supposed to be back soon, so I'll get at the buyer and find out what day he supposed to be here."

"Yeah, do that." We slapped hands. Tone was doing his best to ease up out of there, but I stopped him quick. "Tone, don't forget our conversation."

"I'm on it." Tone's response was just a tad bit too quick for me, but he could have that. In the next seventy-two hours, he had a lot to prove.

"On the way out, pick up that trash from the side of the road." If he thought he was getting a free pass, grits wasn't grocery. "You gotta earn your money some kind of way, since you can't hustle. I probably should just hire you as the groundskeeper, or the maintenance man or some shit."

"You wild." Chris laughed.

The sound of the door and female giggles caught our attention. All three of our heads swiveled in their direction and Coop was coming inside with two brown-skinned females.

"Damn." I looked up at Chris and he was cheesing his ass off.

"Quit slobbing, nigga."

"Them ho's fine as fuck." He looked down at me. "Say they ain't."

"They straight, but I only have eyes for my woman. When you get older, you'll understand that." I tried schooling him, but I knew that shit went in one ear and out the other. Chris was still young, so he thought with his dick instead of his brain.

"Fuck all that. I think I just found my next baby mama." Chris sat down in the chair adjacent to me.

Coop walked up with them on his heels. "Bruh, meet Sparkle and Star. They sisters."

"Well, that's obvious if they twins, fool." The first one had long red hair and red lipstick. She approached me and extended her hand out to me, so I grabbed it. "I'm Brick."

"Brick's a strong name and it's nice to meet you. I must say that I wasn't expecting you to be so fine." She licked her lips seductively. "Don't see why you need help finding any woman."

All I could do was laugh because she was misinformed. "Yeah, I don't have that problem."

"Hmm. Okay." She smiled.

"Well, I'm Star." Star eased between me and took my hand. She was wearing blue hair with blue lipstick.

"So, y'all ain't gone introduce me?" Chris spoke up. In all honesty, I forgot he was there.

"That's Chris and he was just leaving." I dismissed him quickly.

"Damn, that's fucked up." The disappointment was all over his face and in his voice.

Chris stood up and both girls laughed. "Hi, Chris. Bye, Chris." They joked. He was so pissed he walked straight out the door in silence.

Coop walked over and sat down. "So, what you think?"

"They look good," I answered truthfully. "So how do we tell y'all apart besides the obvious?"

"We'll show you," Sparkle replied all bubbly and shit.

Both girls placed their handbags on the table and turned their backs to me. As I watched closely, both sisters pulled the matching jeans they were wearing down to their ankles and stepped out of them. They didn't have on a single pair of panties. I grinned and looked at Coop, 'cause they had some phat asses tucked in them tight ass pants. He had this devilish grin on his face. Sparkle had a big-ass butterfly on her cheeks. She clapped them while glancing at me over her shoulder to make sure I was looking. The wings flapped gracefully like it was ready to take off on her ass.

Star had lips and a tongue on her ass. When she clapped them her cheeks moved rapidly, along with the tongue. She bent all the way over and grabbed her ankles showing her pussy. I couldn't lie, that shit made my dick hard just looking at it. Star was in competition with her sister for my attention and I peeped that out the gate. She eased down into a split and bounced her ass up and down carefully, so she didn't touch the floor.

"A'ight, ladies, I see what y'all working with and it's very nice. However, is there anything else that I could see to tell y'all apart? Since I won't be looking at y'all asses on a daily basis." I kept my composure, as temptation whispered in my ear.

The twins stood up, sauntered over to me and straddled each leg. They rubbed my chest and whispered nasty shit in my ear. "Can you handle both of us, Zaddy?" Sparkle whispered.

Star grabbed my dick and licked her lips. "He definitely can, sis. It's enough for the both of us."

It was tempting, but I had to push them away. "Believe me, if I was single I'd fuck both of y'all, but I have a woman." As soon as they backed up, I rose to my feet. "Get dressed so we can discuss the job description."

I signaled Coop. "I'll be right back."

"Yeah." Coop laughed since he knew firsthand I was doing my best not to cheat on my girl.

Quickly escaping a moment of infidelity, I rushed in the direction of the bathroom to jack my dick. Zuri deserved my faithfulness and loyalty, so I had to handle my business solo until I got home. And, I didn't want to catch blue balls around this bitch.

Chapter 16

Zuri

The more I sat in the house, I was becoming lazier by the day and that wasn't normal for me. My days consisted of snacks, naps and trash TV. It had been so long since I did this and I must've watched damn near every episode of *Cheaters, Paternity Court and Maury.* Some of the shit people did on camera for the world to see was ridiculous, but I couldn't deny that it was funny as hell.

By the time Wednesday rolled around, I was ready to get out the house. My eyes wanted to see the sun and get some fresh air. I missed going to work and seeing some of my co-workers. They had been calling, but I wasn't up to conversing with anyone. Jason had been calling and texting, but I wasn't answering for obvious reasons.

Brick left early that morning, so I was alone until he returned. I wasn't due to return to work for another two weeks, but I had to get out of there. One more day of being non-active was going to result in me going foolish and getting fat. Especially since I was with child, eating reckless and not exercising. The closest I got to a workout was having sex and climbing the stairs.

My mind was made up, so I decided to get up and get dressed for work, just in case Brick came back early. The first stop was the shower and to brush my teeth and wash my face. After my quick session, I scurried to the bedroom and threw on the first dress I spotted in the closet. It was a fitted dress, but I had plenty of room to breathe, even with my little pudge. The building was normally cold, so I grabbed my cardigan, purse and pistol. Brick had been on high alert when it boiled down to my safety, so to keep him from fussing I tucked it into my bag and rushed out the door.

Traffic was so smooth to the point I made it to work in a little under ten minutes. There was a shortcut by my house that I rarely took, because I preferred the scenic route. When I walked into the building, the first person to greet me was Jason. He was strolling down the hallway in a zone until he looked up and saw my face. The way his eyes lit up let me know that I was truly missed.

"Zuri," he shouted and sprinted in my direction to hug me. "I'm so sorry for your loss. I've been trying to reach you for weeks."

Our embrace was tight and longer than usual, but I needed that hug. It had been a long and exhausting road for me and with me being absent I knew they would be concerned, once I finally decided to come back. A trip down memory lane wasn't what I wanted and they needed to respect my wishes of the sensitive, yet fresh traumatic experience that I've gone through.

"I know, but I was in no condition to talk," I explained with my head resting on his chest.

"I understand." Jason rocked me in his arms for a few more seconds before letting me go. "Why did you come back so soon? I thought you had at least another week or two left."

"I do, but I couldn't stay in that house another day. All I do is binge watch trash television and eat snacks all day. It's downright depressing and unhealthy, to say the least."

Jason looked me up and down and smiled. "Yeah, I see. You even picked up a little belly while you were away."

His comment made me react and place my hand on my stomach. "This is just baby fat."

Jason's mouth dropped and his eyes fell back onto my little pudge. I didn't want to tell him in that way, but it was out now and I could see the disappointment in his eyes. That wasn't even his reaction when he saw Brick, but I was sure he was thinking that whatever chance he had with me was completely over.

"Wow!" Jason reached out and placed his hand on mine. "So, you let him get you pregnant, huh?"

"You say it like he trapped me." Now he had me a little on the defensive side.

"I'm just saying, he is a little controlling, so it's possible that he wants to make sure you are off the market."

"Jason, I understand why you would say that and I have apologized for his behavior that night. But, contrary to your belief, Brandon is a really good person and he's sweet." No man could ever come for mine without me defending him.

"Yeah, I saw that."

"Sarcasm isn't your strong point." In a defensive stance I rocked on my heels with my arms at my side. "And let me say this, he has never put his hands on me and he treats me the way a man should treat his woman. He was the only person that stood by me when I needed a shoulder to cry on."

This conversation was not what I expected from Jason and it was obvious he was upset about my pregnancy, but that wasn't his concern. It wasn't like I gave him false hope at a relationship with me, so he had no right to go there period.

"Well, if you would've answered your phone, I could've been there for you as well." He shrugged his shoulders. "I guess it makes sense as to why you didn't answer for me."

"Let's just end this conversation right now before I say something I won't regret. It was nice seeing you, Jason." I turned to walk away, but he grabbed my arm.

"Zuri, I'm sorry."

"Sure you are." I snatched away from him and stormed off in the direction of my office.

The door was locked, as it should be, so I put my key inside and turned the knob. Just as I stepped inside and prepared to close the door, Jason was coming in behind me.

"Get out of my office," I snapped.

"No, wait. I need you to hear me out." Jason closed the door and stepped close to me, invading my personal space, but I backed up. "Zuri, you know that I want nothing but the best for you and that my intentions with you were always good from the beginning."

He paused and rubbed his hand over his face. "Hearing that you are pregnant just really messed me up, because I knew that I would get a chance with you. But, now I know it will never happen."

My extra sensitive ass just stood there, as tears began to flood my vision. Jason was a really good dude and he deserved someone that was equally yoked. He knew nothing about my past and I didn't want to tarnish what we had by inviting him into that part of my life. Now that I knew better and was taking the necessary steps to get away from Daman, our actions made me feel embarrassed and dirty whenever I thought about it.

Jason grabbed my hand and pulled me close to him. "From the bottom of my heart, I am sorry for what I said, but when you love a person and get hit with devastating news you react in a certain way."

Through my teary eyes I could see the sincerity in his eyes, but I couldn't allow that to affect my judgement. "You don't love me, you're just saying that."

"So, you can stand here and honestly say that you don't know how I feel about you?"

Honestly, I did know how he felt, but I wasn't going to answer his question. It was irrelevant and a little too late for any of it. I was in love with Brick and there was no changing my mind. He was my one true love and possessed the qualities I wanted and needed in a man. His dominance is what attracted me to him in the first place. I'm submissive by nature, so I need a man that will lead. Brick is the decision maker and my provider, and I trust him to lead me in the right direction. Jason just wasn't hard enough for me. He was too much of a pushover.

"Zuri, I've loved you since the day you said hello to me. There was something so special in the way you spoke those words and I knew that we were meant for each other, but you didn't believe that. Now that I know where we stand, I won't push the envelope and I'll just love you from afar. We can still be friends of course, but I will respect your relationship."

That's all I wanted him to do, respect my decisions and relationship. "Thank you," I whispered.

"I'll always be here if you need me, okay?"

"Okay."

"Lunch later?" Jason released me from his hold.

"Of course." I smiled.

We were still friends and there was no harm in going to lunch with him.

"Be ready at one."

"I'll be ready."

When he walked out, I closed the door and went to have a seat at my desk and took a deep breath. Then, I opened up my purse to get my compact mirror, so I could check my face and clean myself up. After I was done, I turned on my computer so I could get started with my day.

Over the next few hours, I checked all of my emails and listened to my voicemails. I was buried to my neck in that mess. My manager handled my caseload while I was away and kept me abreast of what was going on. She had sent me a very long and descriptive email about the individuals under my care. In the midst of me working, my phone rang, so I answered it.

"What's up, baby?"

"What you doing?" Brick asked.

"Working."

"Working where?" His voice was a little high-pitched at that point, but he wasn't yelling.

"My job," I calmly stated.

Brick sighed. "Zuri, why did you go back to work? You not ready for that yet."

"I can't stay in that house another day. I'm bored and about to go crazy. It's not like you there with me all day and I'm getting lazy. That's not me, baby."

"You right, but I wish you would've called me first before you snuck off. What time you going to lunch?"

Immediately, I remembered that Jason was taking to me to lunch. "I'm not sure yet, but you don't have to come. I have a lot of work on my desk, so I probably won't take a lunch. I'll just grab something from the machine until I get home."

"Nah, you need to eat some food. I'll bring you something." He wasn't taking no for an answer.

"Baby, it's okay. I'm not that hungry and I'm not staying for my whole shift. I just needed to get out the house for a few hours."

"Okay. Well, I'll see you when you get off. I'll probably beat you there."

"I love you."

"I love you too."

As soon as I disconnected the call, like clockwork, Daman was calling. I swear, he picked the right time to fuck up my day. We hadn't spoken since I'd texted him about Legend's murder. Every call or text I ignored, but today I wanted to talk to him.

"Hello."

"You finally answered my call. I thought I was gone have to send somebody to check on you. What's going on with you?" Daman was strangely calm and I had to admit, it was a little unsettling.

"Nothing. I'm okay."

"You sure about that?"

"Yes, I am."

"I know dealing with this alone probably has you drained, but I want you to know that I'm here for you. Whatever you need, just let me know and I got you." Daman probed like he was fed information and fishing for an answer.

"I'm not dealing with this alone and I told you that I'm fine. I just needed some time to myself to mentally process the idea of losing my brother at the hands of some idiot."

"So, who's been with you?" Daman made me feel like this was an interrogation.

"Why are you asking me all these questions?" That made me pause and think back to when Brick said he saw a man sitting across the street from the house.

"Can I just be concerned about who's been keeping my baby company? I mean I do have a right to know."

"Nobody, so you can stop probing now."

"So, who is Brick?" he blurted out. "That's who been by your side during your time of need?"

It was obvious he had been speaking to someone and knowing Daman, that was probably one of his men outside of my house. He had already said he was concerned. "How do you know about him?"

"So, he does exist? Hmm." He paused for a second and I remained silent, because I knew he was about to say something else slick. "And, is this the guy you was fucking while I was on the phone?"

"Yes."

"He's been around for a while now. You must like him a lot if you letting him stay in the house with you. That's your boyfriend?"

I wasn't sure if it was sarcasm or him slipping into a father role for a moment, which was something that barely happened. Daman had more information than expected and there was no point in lying, especially if I wanted to be free from him. The truth was going to come out eventually and it might as well be me that delivered the news to him.

"I'm just going to be honest with you. Hopefully, this will answer all of the questions you are about to spit at me."

"I want to look in your eyes while you talk to me."

"That's fine."

"I'm about to call you on video."

Daman hung up the phone and called me right back. Over the years he'd managed to keep himself up and he still looked the same. Handsome as ever. We stared at one another for at least a minute with no words spoken. Finally, I propped the phone up so I didn't have to hold it.

"Okay, this is hard for me, but it has to be said and executed."

I took a deep breath and sighed. This was going to be the most heart wrenching news I delivered to Daman and there was nothing he could say or do to change my mind. This time, I was standing on my word and decision. Persuasion was not an option, now or in the future.

"First, I just want to say that I love you beyond the moon and stars aligned in the sky. The love you have shown has been nothing less of amazing, but you and I both know that it's wrong the way we carried on for all of these years. I'm not blaming you, because when I realized it was wrong, I didn't do anything about it because it felt so right in my eyes. In case you are wondering, no I am not upset with you, I don't have a reason to be. Not once have you done anything to hurt me physically."

Daman observed me in silence with hands propped underneath his chin. Occasionally, he would nod his head to let me know he was listening to my every word.

"I have a lot of girls on my case that have been in my shoes, but they weren't willing participants. However, my situation was different. I wanted to be with you sexually after seeing the way Legend displayed his affection towards Shakira when I was younger. I wanted to feel that same love and that was why I came into your room that night. When you dismissed me, I was heartbroken and I know as a father, I made you feel bad about doing so and I somewhat hated you for that."

My emotions were starting to kick in, but I fought hard to keep the tears from falling to avoid weakness.

"You succumbed to my wants because you wanted to be the best father, but it was wrong and you should've stood your ground with me. As an adult you knew better, but again, I don't blame you and I want to apologize to you on my behalf. My decision has been a long time coming, and it's because I've battled with myself on a daily basis about letting go the one I've loved all my life. You were my first in everything I did, so that made everything a little more difficult."

Daman seemed dazed and wounded by my words, but I was on a roll and I couldn't allow his emotions or hard stare deter me from my mission.

"Brick and I have been dating for a few months now and I actually love him. He's what I need right now and he treats me right, so you don't have to worry about that."

Daman shook his head in disapproval. "You don't know him to love him in such a short amount of time. You just saying that because you want to get away from me."

"I do," I objected. He was not about to derail my emotions or try to convince me that what I felt for Brick weren't real.

"And, he loves me too. Not only does he tell me, but he shows me on a daily basis. The things you did for me and to me are one in the same. You taught me about the love of a man and how he responds and treats the woman he loves. Brick does all of those things we discussed and you should be happy that I found someone doing the things he should be doing."

142

"I didn't tell you those things for you to find that in another man. I did it so you wouldn't question the love I have for you. Zuri, there is no man walking this planet that will do what I've done for you, and you need to understand that."

"You're sadly mistaken because I found that in him and that's why I am ending things with you. What we shared is over and I am moving on with my life. I need you to respect that and not try to convince me to stay."

"Zuri, I love you," he pleaded.

"Please," I said just above a whisper. "Don't do this to me. Just let me go. If you don't want me to hate you, then you'll let me go."

I could feel myself getting soft, but my inner conscience told me to keep going. "If you truly love me the way you say you do, then let me be happy with him. You've had me all my life and I want out of this relationship forever. I'm getting older and I want to start a family with this man."

"Damn, that nigga got some good-ass game. More than Kevin. He couldn't get you away from me and you were with him for two years." He could see the surprise in my face. "Yeah, I knew about him and we both know how I got that info."

Daman knew about Kevin because I told him, but he didn't know the seriousness of our relationship or the length of it. There was only one person behind that and it was Kyra.

"I'm not worried about that, period. After I found out about the two of y'all, it all made sense about some of the things you knew about me on the outside. Did she tell you that she fucked Kevin too? I'm sure she didn't mention that to you."

"I don't give a fuck about Kyra and you know that for a fact. My only concern is you."

"That may be true, but you don't have to worry about me because I'm in good hands now. Brick takes care of all my wants and needs, so I'm going to be okay."

"For now. He'll show you his true colors sooner or later." Daman bit down on his bottom lip and nodded his head. "And, I'll be here when he does because I'm not going anywhere."

"As a father and grandfather you can, but that's it. We are over and I'm serious about it."

Daman grabbed his phone, as if he was grabbing me physically and looked at me through hooded eyes. "You better not let him get you pregnant and I mean that shit."

"It's too late, because I'm carrying his child now."

"Stop lying, 'cause you starting to piss me off."

"I'm not." I stood up, so he could see my stomach. "It's the truth and we are going to be a family."

"Nah, that's the dress. I don't believe you."

To put an end to his disbelief, I raised my dress and turned to the side. When I pulled it back down and took my seat, his head was held low. Daman needed a minute to process what he saw, so I sat there in silence until he raised his head. Tears were welled up in his eyes and they had started to fall. He was hurt, but I couldn't do anything about it. I refused to pacify him and his reactions.

Daman's next words were inevitable. "Zuri, you need to have an abortion."

"No, I don't. I love him and we are going to be together. Please understand that this," I pointed my finger between the both of us, "is over between us. I'm not asking for permission. I'm telling you."

"So, that's it, huh?"

"Yes, and now I need time away from you. After I hang up, don't call me or I'm going to change my number. Once I get myself together, I will call you when I'm ready to talk. I'm hoping that in the future, we can have a father and daughter relationship only. Nothing else."

"I'm sorry too and I still love you." Daman wiped his eyes. "If you never hear from me again, just know that you signed my death certificate."

Daman hung up the phone.

There was a knock on the door. "Come in," I shouted.

Jason walked in with a huge smile on his face. "You ready for lunch?"

"As a matter of fact, I am. I'm starving. Let's go." I grabbed my things and we left.

Chapter 17

Brick

IHOP was unusually crowded for it to be a weekday, but I guessed everyone wanted breakfast for lunch. I walked up to the counter and interrupted the host that was too busy running her mouth to notice a paying customer.

With a sigh of irritation, I dropped my keys on the counter. "Pick up for Brick and quit all that gossiping on the company clock."

She immediately stopped talking and turned to face me. "Excuse me?" The look on her face was priceless, but her unit turned into a smile when she saw me. "Pops, you trying to get me fired? And how did you know that it was me?"

"Nah. I can't have that. Then you gone start asking me for money and I know that peanut head from anywhere."

Janae laughed, showing the braces I paid for. "You so petty, bruh. I swear."

"Yeah, I know. Why I haven't I heard from you? I heard you have a boyfriend now."

Janae rolled her eyes. "Oh, my goodness. Who told you that, Mommy?"

"Don't worry about that. Just answer the question."

"Yeah, I do."

"I need to meet him and y'all better not be having sex either." Janae knew I was serious when it came to her. Being protective of the ones I loved was one of my strongest traits.

One of her co-workers started laughing with her nosey ass and walked up to her. Janae's bright cheeks became rosy. "This is so embarrassing. You do know I'll be eighteen soon."

"No, it's not, girl. That's what daddies do." She stood at the register. "Boo, slide over please. I need to ring up a customer."

Janae was happy for the interruption. "I'm going to get your order. I'll be right back."

"Yeah."

I looked down at my phone and realized I needed to move a little bit faster. I would catch Janae on the rebound. She returned quickly and sat my food on the counter. I pulled a stack of bills from my pocket.

"Don't worry about the food. It's cool."

Ignoring her, I peeled off a few fifty-dollar bills and handed them to her. "Happy Birthday."

"It's not until Saturday." She tilted her head to the side.

"I know, but I may not see you that day. So, take it."

Janae took the money from my hand. "His name is Demarcus and he'll be there on Saturday if you want to meet him."

"A'ight."

Janae walked from around the counter and gave me a hug. She was a little taller than Zuri, so we were damn near close in height. The girl was a damn beanstalk. "Thank you and I hope I get to see you on Saturday."

"Make sure you call me."

"I will."

"We'll talk later. I have to go drop this food off to my lady."

"Kiss Bre for me and bring her with you."

"Okay."

It was almost two o'clock, so I grabbed the food and left. Thank God that her job was right up the street.

Janae was my goddaughter, but I hadn't seen her that much since I got out. Her father and I was tight back in the day before he got jammed up on a robbery charge. We crossed paths in the feds and he asked me to keep an eye on her when I got out, so I gave him my word that I would do so.

Zuri's car was still in the parking lot when I pulled up so I was happy I didn't miss her. I wanted to surprise her with lunch since she thought eating junk food from the machine was good enough for my baby. I parked next to her car and got out. There were flowers in one hand and food in the other. She appreciated the small things and that's what I loved about her the most. My baby wasn't concerned about that material shit I gave her.

The receptionist was on the phone when I stepped to the counter, but she addressed me right away with her hand over the receiver. "Give me one moment, please."

The building was cold and fairly quiet. It looked like a big ass daycare center with all of the kiddie graffiti on the walls.

"Hello. Sorry about that. How can I help you?" the receptionist asked.

"I need to see Zuri Monroe."

"Oh, okay. You have a delivery for her?"

My head snapped back. Immediately I felt tried, as if a delivery man would show up looking this damn good. That blind heffa must have bumped her goddamn head. I had to take a deep breath and remember I was at my lady's place of business, to keep from cussing her ass out. "Do I look like a delivery man? I'm her boyfriend and I would like to see her."

"Oh, I apologize, but Zuri left for lunch about an hour ago."

"You sure about that, because her car is outside?"

"Maybe she rode with someone, because I saw her leave. Would you like to leave that here and I give it to her?" She reached for the items, but I took a step back.

"No, thanks. I got it." Slowly, I left the building and headed back in the direction of the parking lot so I could wait on her. Whoever she rode with had to park, so I was sure I wouldn't miss her, but to be on the safe side, I decided to call her.

My hands were full so I stopped and sat the flowers down on the step and dug in my pocket for my phone. She was on speed dial, so I hit one button to dial her number. The phone rang for a while before going to voicemail.

"She'll call back." I put my phone away, picked up the flowers and walked off.

When I hit the corner, I saw a dude walking to the passenger door of his car, so I stood there and waited to see who was getting out. The seconds it took for the person to get out was long enough for sweat beads to form on my forehead. Then lo and behold, Zuri got out of the car and her smile was big enough for me to see all of her teeth from a distance. Apparently, she wanted to depart from her muthafuckin' smile and teeth in her mouth, because I was two seconds away from knocking them down her throat.

I moved swiftly like a lion hunting his prey and by the time she looked up, I was a foot away from her. Zuri's eyes stretched out her head like she was morphing or some shit. All of her movements came to a halt, even the laughter. The smile she was wearing a moment ago was hanging low to the concrete.

"Pick ya' jaw up, baby." My face was balled up and I dared Urkel to utter one single word. He was irrelevant because Zuri was my woman and she knew what I told her about being around the nigga. With no regards to the items in my hand, I crossed my arms.

"Baby, I—"

She tried to speak, but I cut her off. "So this why you couldn't answer my call? You went to lunch with this nigga?"

"Brandon, it's not like that. I'm just being a friend," Jason spoke up in her defense.

"Lunch been over, so you better go clock in before you get wrote up. This between me and my lady." Jason walked off without another word.

"Brick, please don't be upset with me. It's not what you think." Zuri rocked on her heels like she had to pee.

"What do I think, Zuri?"

"That I was doing something, but I wasn't. I promise." Zuri tried pleading her case, but there was no need to because she disregarded everything I told her.

"I'm far from insecure and I know you didn't do anything with him, because you would be stupid to do so, but you disobeyed me. When I caught you last time I told you that I better not catch you with that nigga again. Did I not?"

"I did, but..." Suddenly, she choked up like she was ready to start crying, like that was going to sway me.

I leaned down in her face. "But what?"

Zuri wiped those crocodile tears and sniffled. "I became emotional about my brother and he offered to take me to lunch, just to take my mind off of things."

148

"Well, he did good at that because a moment ago you were skinning and grinning, but when I show up, you start crying. That's funny as hell. You steady trying to run game on me like I'm soft or some shit."

Zuri was lucky I didn't snap the way I normally would. The thought crossed my mind, but she was under enough stress and I didn't want her to miscarry. Instead I kept my composure. It was all good though, because I had a solution for all of that.

"I'm not trying you," she said softly.

"But, did I not tell you to stay away from him?"

"You did and I'm sorry. It wasn't like that." Zuri held her stomach and began to whimper. That girl thought she was slicker than oil, trying to use the baby to keep me from getting on her ass. She had another thing coming and a lot more to learn about Brick, but I decided to play her game.

"What's wrong? Why you holding your stomach?"

"I don't feel good." She bent forward and I wanted to laugh so bad, because she was really carrying on badly.

"You should've stayed your ass home like I told you to. It's okay though you can get plenty of rest. Let's go inside and get your stuff."

Zuri froze and stood up quickly. "I don't want you to cause a scene here. I'll be right back."

"Nah. I'm good."

"So you're not mad?"

"Nope, but you about to be."

She stopped and looked at me with her face scrunched up. "Why you say that?"

"Because, you quitting your job. Now let's go before I really cause a scene."

"Why?" she whined.

"Sick women shouldn't be working. They need to be in the house with their feet up, relaxing and making sure their families are straight."

"That's not fair."

"Life isn't fair and sometimes we have to do things we don't want to do. I asked you to stay away from him, you promised me you would, but you lied. So now, we doing it my way."

Zuri knew I was dead-ass serious, which is why she didn't say a word on the way in the building. I followed her to her office, watched her write the letter of resignation and pack up her office. That shit was dead. When I said don't talk to a muthafucka, that's exactly what I meant.

***

The resentment Zuri had towards me two days ago for making her quit her job had suddenly faded away. I guess she had come to terms that what I said went. It was my way, or no way at all. The way she chose to handle it was all on her, 'cause I wasn't bending or folding and the quicker she realized that, the better. It was a different story if I wasn't providing for her, but I was. Anything that needed to be done, I did it. Anything that needed to be paid, I footed the bill and I demanded respect. It was blatant disrespect for her to be riding in the car with a nigga I told her to stay away from. If I wasn't out here entertaining bitches, she needed to do the same and that's real.

Now, the softer part of me did care about the way I reacted to the situation, but it was for a good reason. My woman needed to listen to me and stay in her place. Bad things were liable to happen whenever I was disobeyed. Shit could've went left quick and if she was a different female I would've beat that ass at her job, but with Zuri it was different. I didn't see it in myself to put my hands her. I loved her too much to hurt her physically. Before I hit her I would walk away and I put that on my mama. Unless she did some foul ass shit that warranted me to lay hands.

Since Zuri was home full-time, that gave me more time with Breanna during the week. Normally, I would get her on the weekends, because I didn't have to take her to school. I'm in and out on the weekdays and I can't have my daughter out and about with me or ripping and running all night. And besides, she needed some practice with a child anyway. I pulled up at the Dunkin Donuts on Sunrise, by Dillard High School and parked my car.

"They put a Dunkin Donuts in the hood," I said to myself laughing. Back in the day, I remembered when this very spot was Captain Crabs. Times surely had changed and they were doing their best to move the blacks out the neighborhood. Slowly, but surely, they continued to upgrade and make our area look like a tourist attraction.

It was empty on the inside, so it was easy to spot who I was looking for. She was sitting in the corner, looking through her phone. I walked up and sat down across from her.

"Thanks for meeting me."

"No problem. What's going on?" she asked.

Before I saw her at the funeral, I never realized how much Mehzani and Zuri looked alike. Maybe that's why she looked familiar to me.

"Well, as you know, your sister has been going through a lot and that's the reason she hasn't called you yet. She tried to go back to work two days ago, but she had a breakdown and had to leave. The plan was for me to take her on a trip, but I can't do that now. My schedule won't allow it, but I was hoping that you would accompany her. That would give y'all a chance to catch up and work on the relationship you lost over the years."

Mehzani sat there and fidgeted with her keys before she finally looked at me. "That sounds like a really good idea, but Gucci is still in the hospital and I don't know if he's going to pull through."

"I understand that, but his condition won't change overnight and you can't stop what's meant to be. All you're going to do is make yourself sick thinking about it. It's a waiting game right now and I believe this trip will be beneficial for you too."

"Yeah, that's true, but I'm scared I might lose him if I leave," Mehzani's voice was low when she spoke. That told me she was unsure on what she wanted to do. One thing for sure, she was just like her sister in so many ways.

"You can't stop God's plan for him. You're not there now and he could be taking his last breath as we speak. You get my drift?"

Mehzani nodded her head.

"Listen, I'm not trying to tell you what to do, but I would love for you and your sister to get together. That would mean so much to her." My eyes drifted to the clear glass, looking out into the traffic, as I stroked my beard. "Zuri needs you right now and to be honest, I'm concerned about her."

"Why is that?" That part caught her attention, like I knew it would.

"She's pregnant and I'm concerned about my baby. I just want her to go away and have some fun. You know take her mind off of things."

Mehzani's eyes lit up in excitement. "Aww, she's having a baby. How far is she?"

"Two months and I would like for her to have a safe and healthy pregnancy. I don't want her to miscarry."

"Okay," she replied, but I wasn't sure what that meant.

"The trip will be paid in full and I'll give you some spending money, so you won't have to come out of pocket. If you need some time to think about this, then hit me up."

I grabbed my keys and prepared to get up, but Mehzani stopped me. "Brick, wait."

"Yeah."

"I'll go. Just let me know when."

"I appreciate that. I'll call you in a few hours with the info."

"Okay."

That was good news and I was happy she agreed to go. Zuri needed to get away and I owed it to her. If it wasn't for me, she wouldn't be in the predicament she was in, but that was water under the bridge and all I could do was keep on pushing.

Chapter 18

Mehzani

After speaking with Brick, my mood slightly changed. I was happy about reuniting with my sister, but I was still down about my man. It felt strange going on a trip and having fun while he was in the hospital, but I wanted my sister back more than anything in the world. I was surprised when he hit me up, because I expected Zuri to be on the receiver. Ever since he gave me that phone I waited patiently, silently praying that she would call. With Zuri back in my life, it would be complete. At this point in my life, she and Gucci were the ones that mattered to me the most. The problem with that was I didn't know if he would return to me and make me complete once again, but I was hopeful to say the least.

The day Gucci flatlined was the worst feeling in the world. It felt like someone snatched my heart out my chest and stomped on it repeatedly. One of the nurses told us he had coded, but a miracle happened and his heart started beating again, but very weakly. I knew it was no one but God. He had a plan for Gucci's life, so death wasn't an option. At least, I hoped so. I had my skeletons in my closet, sometimes I didn't even understand why I was being punished so hard, but I always believed in the man upstairs.

The thought of not knowing what really happened that night was scary as hell. I didn't know if I was safe or not. Melvin's plan was to stay with me until he got to the bottom of the situation, or until Gucci's condition was better. I guess it was safe to say that he was my bodyguard.

During our short time together, we got the chance to learn more about each other. Melvin was a really cool dude and I could see why Gucci was drawn to him. I also found out that he was only twenty-three, with five kids and a baby boy he didn't get to see. That sounded a lot like Gucci's situation. It was funny, because they had so much in common.

Apparently, the mother didn't want him involved in the child's life. Melvin was brown-skinned with a brush cut and very appealing to the eyes, but I wasn't interested in him. I was merely stating a fact. I liked my men just a little more rugged like Gucci, brown-skinned with long dreads and a mouth full of golds. Sadness came over me, because I missed him so much.

Melvin interrupted my thoughts. "Earth to Mehzani," he laughed, while waving his arms in front of my face.

"I'm sorry." A heavy painful sigh escaped my lips. "I was just thinking about Gucci. Do you think he's going to make it?"

"I hope so, but he's not doing too well, so we probably should prepare ourselves for the worst."

"Yeah, that's what I'm afraid of. I don't know what I would do without him. He got me on the right track and now this." I pulled my knees to my chest and wrapped my arms around my legs. "I might as well go back to the trenches of where I came from."

"No, you won't, because that's not what he wanted for you. If anything happens to him I will be here for you, so don't worry about it. I promise."

Melvin seemed sincere, but I didn't really know him like that to believe he would actually help me. It sounded good, but I would take everything he said with a grain of salt. "You would do that for me?"

"I would do it for him, because he really loves you, man. You have no idea. Why do you think he told us to stop serving you? I ain't gone lie when he first said it I thought he was crazy, but when he broke it down I understood."

"Understood what?"

"I can't tell you, but just know that it's all good."

It didn't make sense to mention it if he wasn't going to elaborate on, but I let it go because I was certain he wasn't going to tell me anyway. "Have you heard from his cousin, Brick? Has he heard anything?"

I didn't know Brick well enough to question him, so I decided to ask Mel, since we were a little closer.

"Nah, I haven't. He's been MIA since the shooting. The streets hot right now, so I haven't heard anything from him just yet. I'll keep you in the loop if I find out anything though."

"You don't think it was him, do you?" Mel wasn't very good at eye contact, because they shifted when I mentioned Brick.

"That's his cousin. Why would you think that?"

"I don't know." I shrugged my shoulders. "I'm just asking questions because I want answers. I don't know what happened to him or nothing. The police have no leads and I don't know if I'm a target or not. It's nerve wrecking and that's why I don't go anywhere."

"Well you safe here. Gucci made sure that no one knew where he lived except for me." Mel looked me in the eyes for the first time and held his glance. "I told you that I got you and I'm not gone let anything happen to you." His tone was soothing and that was what I needed at that very moment.

Melvin and I spent the remainder of the day in the house, watching Netflix. The same way Gucci and I used to do. I missed him so much and I had been praying daily he would get better, but nothing was happening. His condition was the same. The waiting game was making me so emotional that I cried every single day, but at least I had someone there to wipe my tears away.

"Are you going to drink that whole bottle?" Melvin was downing some Hennessy straight out the bottle, while I sipped on my Patrón.

"Don't get mad at me because you drink slow. You better catch up." Mel took a pull of his blunt and exhaled the smoke.

"Let me hit that." I got up and sat beside him on the floor.

"I don't think you should be smoking." He stretched his arm to the side of him to keep me from grabbing it.

"Why not? I'm an adult and I'm stressing right now. I need to relax and take my mind off of my issues."

Melvin thought about it for a few minutes. "You right, here." He passed me the blunt and I took a pull from it. The weed was so strong I choked right off the bat.

"Damn, you got virgin lungs now?" He joked. "My man got yo' ass on the straight and arrow, huh?"

"Yeah, he do," I said in between coughs. "I haven't smoked a blunt in a while now and if I wasn't so damn stressed I wouldn't be smoking it now. I've been drinking more than usual too. It's like every day, I buy a bottle."

"Damn, sis. You going through it."

"You have no idea." I took another pull, but that time I didn't choke. My ass got lightheaded when I inhaled, swallowed and blew it through my nose. That shit was potent as hell.

"First, my brother got killed a few weeks ago and then, my man got shot. This shit is too crazy for me. It's like, you never realize how bad shit is until the Grim Reaper comes to your front door, knocking and snatches up your loved ones."

Just hearing those words made me realize how important it was for Zuri and me to get close. We spent so many years apart without knowing what the other was going through. Friends, in my book, were limited. I didn't trust females and they didn't make them ho's solid like they used to. That was the number one reason why I was always surrounded by a bunch of dudes. No drama or that backstabbing shit. There was so much shit that happened to me in my past that I could write a book on the many situations I was forced to face alone. Hopefully, that would end when Zuri and I took this trip. The phone Brick gave me was on the coffee table and I was waiting for it to ring.

"Damn, Legend was your brother?"

I picked up my glass of liquor and downed it. "Yeah."

"Sorry for your loss." Melvin took another swig from his bottle. "That's fucked up what happened to him. These niggas out here taking all the solid niggas out and they don't give a fuck about who they hurting in the process."

"Tell me about it." Out of the blue, I started bawling hysterically. I mean, there was no warning, no build-up of tears or nothing. Just some random, drop-of-the-dime type of shit. I needed more chaser, so I got up and went to the kitchen.

Melvin was talking to me, but I couldn't hear nothing he was saying. I had to be drunk because I was walking and crying and steady trying to get drunk. The couch tripped me on my way back to my seat and I fell down to my knees.

My security guard jumped up and grabbed me. "Girl, you okay?"

That nigga looked like he had two heads, so I started laughing. "I'm good. Shit. Is you okay?"

"I'm good."

"Good." My head wobbled. "So am I." My bottle was calling my name, so I reached for it. Melvin was a little quicker than me and snatched it up.

"Man, you crazy as hell if you think I'm gone let you keep on drinking. Yo' ass is slumped. Go lay down or something."

Melvin didn't realize that his bottle was in arm's reach when he turned his back, so I grabbed it and turned it up to my mouth. By the time he turned around, I was downing his shit.

"What you doing?"

"You took my drink, so I took yours." My speech was slurred to the max, but I felt so good.

"Don't worry about it, 'cause that's your last drink." Mel grabbed his bottle from me and drank some more.

"Okay, I won't do it again," I lied. As soon as he went to the bathroom or kitchen, I was on that bottle's ass.

"I know because I'm gone pour out the rest if you try and take it. You almost fucked ya' own ass up on that table."

"Just give me back my bottle. You can't stop me from drinking." I pointed a finger in his face. "Number one, I'm grown and number two, I'll just drink when I leave here every day and then you can explain how I got a DUI, or how I was involved in a vehicular homicide crash."

"Yo' ass crazy, but you right tho'."

"I know and I'm not hurting anybody."

"Fine." Melvin gave me back my bottle and I poured up quick.

We sat on the floor and finished watching *Fruitvale Station*. It was on the part where Oscar was shot in the station, so I was crying all over again. Mel looked at me and laughed.

"Man, you are such a crybaby."

"I can't help it."

"Come on, little crybaby, you can lay by me." Mel had his back against the couch with his arm extended out, so I scooted beside him, resting my head on his shoulder.

"And, it's not funny." I pouted like a big-ass baby.

"I told you don't drink that shit, but you hardheaded."

"I miss him so much, Mel. You don't understand."

"I do and I miss my nigga too."

When I looked up into his eyes I could see the sincerity in them. Tears were in mine as we stared at each other long enough for me to feel a little weird about how close we were. Mel wiped my eyes with his thumb, as he whispered in my ear.

"I'm here for you. No matter how long it takes. Everything is going to be okay."

All I could hear was Gucci speaking through him and it rattled my soul. His voice sounded just like his and suddenly I saw Gucci's face replace his. Before I knew it, my lips were on his and we were locked into a deep, passionate kiss. I didn't know what came over me, but I climbed on top and straddled him. Our lips never separated. He grabbed my shoulders and pushed me, interrupting our kiss.

"No, we can't do this," he firmly stated, but I wasn't trying to hear that.

Tears rolled down my face and I felt the rejection shoot through my soul like a bow and arrow. I needed someone and it had to be him. "Please don't push me away," I whispered, as I took off my shirt.

I leaned back down and kissed him again. That time, he didn't reject my advances or push me away like I knew he would. Instead, he went with the flow. We were chest to chest and I could feel his heart beating against mine. The kiss was so intense, I could feel high powered volts of electricity shooting through my body. My hand found its way inside of his gym shorts and pulled out his hard erection. The juices between my legs were soaking the seat of my shorts, so I pulled my PINK shorts to the side and positioned myself over his stiff dick. The tip grazed my clit and it sent chills down my spine. I slid down slowly and he fit me like a glove. A soft moan escaped my lips.

"Mmm."

Mel stuck his hands inside my shorts and squeezed my ass, while pushing me down further onto his lap. Slowly, I winded my hips in a circle like I was grinding to a slow jam. He kept his eyes closed as I rode him steadily. The more I rode him, the more I got into it. My mind drifted off to Gucci and something told me to stop, but we already crossed that line. The dick was deep up in me and there was no point in stopping. Biting down on my lip, I bounced on it hard. A little pain was what I needed, so I could replace the pain I felt in my heart.

"Ooh. Yeah. Ss. Yeah," he moaned, while playing with my nipples with his fingers before slipping them into his mouth. Taking turns sucking on both of my titties with his warm tongue, one of his hands slipped between my legs to play with my clit. It felt good, but I wanted to be pounded on.

"Fuck me," I demanded.

Mel lifted me off of him and placed me onto the floor. As I laid on my back, he pulled off my shorts. Quickly, he removed his shirt, gym shorts and boxers too. Then, he positioned himself between my legs and entered me. My legs were wrapped tightly around his waist. Our kisses were sloppy, yet passionate as he stroked my pussy with a harmonious rhythm. His dick was big as Gucci's and it felt good going in and out of me. Mel took his time as if he was making love to me, but there was no love between us, just two hurt people that loved the same person. My body was yearning for his touch and I needed our bodies to touch, so I slid my arms around his chest area and held him tightly.

"Fuck me hard."

The friction against my clit made it tingle. I wasn't ready to cum yet, so I stuck my hand between legs and used two fingers to open my lips. He was fucking me so good a single tear rolled down the side of my face and dripped into my ear. Those long, fast strokes had me moaning non-stop. Now I understood why he had five kids. That nigga knew exactly what to do to the pussy. I could feel the pressure build up again, so I moved my hand and spread my legs. He used his forearms to hold them up. Melvin used all of his energy to deliver the dick the way I needed him to. He pounded on me hard as fuck for next few minutes.

"Just like that. Just like that." His pelvis slapped against mine with every thrust he delivered. I moaned and whimpered repeatedly, until I creamed heavily on his dick, releasing some built-up pressure.

"Put my legs down." My voice was a little shaky, but he understood what I was saying. Using my forearms, I held my legs open for him. My feet were close to my face. I didn't need to tell him what to do, because he was right back in it the minute I got into position. At first, he was slow stroking me, but that wasn't working for me.

"Fuck me harder than that. Make me scream. I need to feel it in my stomach." I closed my eyes and he followed my instructions. Melvin beat me down like I stole a kilo of cocaine and the plug had a bounty on his head. It was deep in my stomach and it hurt just the way I wanted it to. My mind drifted to another place and I was good with that. It made me feel less guilty. Like I wasn't present or some shit.

A while later, I could feel his body shake and he was stroking me fast, then slow. He was grunting and breathing hard as hell. I needed to cum one more time, so I put my hand on my clit and rubbed it fast until I felt myself about to bust. Mid-stroke, my sex slave pulled out and jacked his dick on my stomach, releasing all of his little babies and laid on the tiled floor beside me.

"Ooh, shit. I'm tired as fuck."

For the next few minutes we laid on the floor in silence, staring at the ceiling. He was probably thinking about his actions the same way I was. Mel finally rolled over onto his knees and got up. Before he walked away, he looked down at me.

"Gucci gone kill me and you," he whispered.

I didn't respond because the damage was already done. We couldn't un-fuck each other. All we could do was move on from what happened. Melvin walked towards the back and I could hear a door close.

My heart sank to my stomach and immediately I felt sick after what he had just said. The guilt kicked in fast and I began to feel queasy. The taste of saliva dripped on the inside of my mouth and I could feel a burp coming. Feet to the floor, I ran to the master bedroom and straight to the bathroom. I got down on my knees and let everything go. Praying to the porcelain God was not what I had in mind for the turn-up. Soon, I lifted my head and took a deep breath.

"You throw up an awful lot. Are you pregnant or something?" Melvin appeared from out of nowhere with the questions.

"I have a weak stomach."

"Yeah, whatever you say. Your phone been ringing." When he walked away, I sat on the floor for a few minutes to collect my thoughts. My cellphone was in the room, so it had to be Brick calling.

Chapter 19

Brick

The trip for Zuri and Mehzani had been booked and paid for. The two siblings would be spending five luxurious days and four nights in sunny Los Angeles, CA, at a beach house. All they had to do was pack and be ready when that flight prepared for takeoff. Hopefully, the trip would make her feel better about what she'd lost in such a short amount of time. It would also make me feel better about the way I handled the situation at her job with Jason. My intentions with her were good from the jump, but there was some shit I didn't play about.

On another note, business was about to be booming in a couple of months, maybe sooner and I had big plans for my family. The Cubans were about to hit me with a bigger shipment and control over some of their territory. Hector was a businessman and a part of one of the most ruthless cartels. It was a pleasure knowing he trusted me enough to let me in. For that, I was grateful and he had my loyalty fa' sho.

We pulled up to the club and I turned off the car. My latest business ventures were in the car with me. I turned in my seat and looked at both of them.

"Listen, when we get in here, I will do all the talking. All you have to do is stand there, look pretty and speak when spoken to. This is a very wealthy man and he wants to be seen with dime pieces on his arm. Understood?"

"Understood, daddy." Sparkle and Star replied in a frisky tone. That shit would've been a turn-on if I was single.

"Let's go."

The three of us walked in like some muthafuckin' stars. I was dressed to the nines as usual and I had the twins to change the color of their hair. My sis, Erin, hooked them up with some jet-black, sexy shit she called a lace front. I didn't know nothing about that fake hair or wigs and shit. It was only right that I broke her off, since she made sure my girls were straight.

Hector was sitting in the back of the club in the VIP section, sipping on some champagne. A wide, devious grin spread across his face. "Brick, my man. What do we have here?"

We shook hands and I sat down across from him. "This is Sparkle and Star."

"It's nice to meet you, beautiful ladies."

Both girls smiled. "The pleasure is ours." Sparkle stepped to him and shook his hand. Star followed her sister's lead.

"I love what I'm seeing." Hector sat back and crossed his legs.

"You asked and I delivered." Making myself comfortable, I sat back and folded my hands in my lap. "Now, let's talk business."

"Of course. Give a minute." He hit the intercom button mounted on the wall beside him. "Miranda, come here. My meeting is about to start."

"Coming, boss." Miranda had to be on standby the way she popped up so quickly. In her hand, she held a silver tray. She walked over to where I was sitting and sat it down in front of me.

"Bon appetit." She smiled.

Hector held a finger in the air. "Miranda, take these lovely ladies to the bar to get a drink on the house."

"Will do. Right this way, ladies." All three women strutted away gracefully and Hector's eyes were glued on his new merchandise.

"Yo." He clapped his hands. "Where the fuck did you find the Doublemint Twins?"

"Ancient Chinese secret."

Since the girls were gone, it was time to get to the matter at hand. I removed the lid on the platter and underneath was a kilo of cocaine. Swiftly, I pulled a knife from my pocket and put a slit in the package. Dipping my finger in it, I rubbed it across my gums and it numbed my mouth instantly.

"High grade."

"Bolivian coke. Straight from the coca plant."

"What's the purity?"

"Ninety-eight percent."

"Hmm." When I flooded the street with this work, I was gone have all these muthafuckas eating from the palm of my hand.

"I'll have my men deliver it to you tonight at ten, so be in place when they get there."

"We'll be in place." Me and Coop was gone be waiting with bells on.

"Oh, I have a question, do you have a number two? This is a lot of work I'm delivering and I need to make sure you meet the quota."

"My number two is in place and I can arrange a sit-down for all of us to meet."

"Okay, now that our drug business is out the way, let's talk about my new merchandise." Hector reached down beside him and grabbed a black bag. "This is for a job well done. Bring me more and there's a lot more where that came from."

He pushed the bag in my direction. When I unzipped it, I came across a lot of bills. It was definitely not what he originally offered. After a moment's reflection of the large sum of cash, he addressed my astonishment.

"It's a lot more than I stated before, but I have some powerful friends in high places and they are interested in your services. In that bag is one hundred thousand dollars, as a startup fee for your services. We need ten more girls and I would like a mixture. All races, so to speak."

"When do you need them by?"

"Over the next few weeks. You can bring them in, I'll approve them and cut you a check. The yellow envelope in there is an incentive for me to take both ladies with me to New York City tonight on my private jet. That should cover the weekend cost."

To verify his claim, I opened up the envelope and there was a check in it for thirty grand. "This is a very generous amount, but why a check?"

"Since we're going to be in business together, I think it's to create some sort of legal paper trail to keep the feds away. Start a legitimate business and open up a business account with that check. It's hard to deposit dirty money without raising suspicions."

"What's the catch? Why you doing all of this for me?" Never in my life have I had a man of Hector's caliber school me on a way to make major bank and without something in return.

Hector was wearing that same devilish smirk on his face as usual. "In the first meeting, I told you I liked you. Like myself, you are an Alpha male and I respect your work ethics. When you came in here, you didn't back down or hold your tongue because of my status. You walked in here with confidence, your head was held high and defended your seriousness about the business. It's not often I say that to anyone, but I respect you as a man."

"I appreciate that." I bowed my head. "I'm looking forward to the future."

"Let's make a toast." Hector poured up two glasses of the finest champagne and handed me one. "To new business ventures."

"To new business ventures." We clinked our glasses together and tossed them back.

***

After the meeting with Hector, I left the girls with him and made my way to my business house to meet Skeet and his homie. An expansion was definitely needed with the shipment coming in, but I needed muthafuckas that wanted to get money without snitching if shit got hot. It was easy to find dealers. They were on every street corner, but loyalty was hard to find. That shit was rare, but I was fortunate to find a few on my team.

Coop was sitting in his car when I pulled up, but he got out when he saw me park. Skeet and his homie was sitting on the porch, looking like some middle school kids up to no good. The way I was feeling after my business meeting, nobody could rain on my parade and that was a fact.

"Whaddup, bruh?" Coop and I hugged.

"Shit, coolin'. Just gettin' off the phone with Danielle crazy ass. Man, I swear she gone drive me crazy," he said in a dry, frustrated tone.

"What the hell she trippin' for now?" Whenever they had issues, I already knew what time it was, but I needed to hear it for myself.

"Same old, not being home bullshit. She wanted to do dinner and a movie tonight, but I told her ass a shipment was coming in and I didn't know how long I was gone be. Then, she started talking about I don't love her and all that fuck shit. I swear, that muhfucka need her head checked."

"Sis crazy and all, but you know she love you." I pointed my finger in his direction. "See, all that cheating you did in the beginning, before the wedding is still fuckin' with her. You know damn well she don't care about you working, especially when she a stay at home wife. She wanna see that money coming in. You gotta make shit right with her. I told you to put a baby in there she'll calm down then."

"Yeah, I hear all that," he replied nonchalantly.

"I'm telling you what I know." I was the female whisperer and he knew that shit. Whenever I was interested in a woman, my strategy was always to get inside their head and heart, before the pussy. After I hit it, she was guaranteed to be fucked up about the kid.

"Bossman, what's good?" Skeet shouted, pointing at his watch. "It's meeting time."

"How many times I have to tell y'all that I'm never late?" I strolled up on him slowly and placed one foot on the step.

"You right," Skeet replied.

His homie looked down at my shoes and nodded his head. I could see the amusement in his eyes, but that was all the young niggas saw. A glamorous lifestyle. "Hell yeah. Balenciaga's. That's what I'm talking about."

"If your main goal is to rock designer, I can tell you right now that you gone fail in this game. Get your money first and you can ball later. Remember that, but in the meantime, let's go inside."

We all went inside to the meeting room. "Have a seat."

Coop and I sat at the head of the table. My fingers were intertwined, resting underneath my chin. "Skeet, you gone introduce us or do I have to do it?"

"I got it." Skeet took a deep breath, taking glances between everyone in the room. Brick and Coop, this is my boy, Kamari, and he ready to get this paper."

"Slow down, man. This a interview and we well aware of what he came here for, but we don't know this nigga." Coop was looking at Skeet, but he immediately turned his attention to Kamari. "What you bringing to the table and is this your first time dealing? Have you popped that hustling cherry yet?"

"Nah, this ain't the first time. When Skeet started dealing for you a while back, I used to accompany him when he hustled. You know make sure nobody was fuckin' wit' my ace. I pretty much have it down packed, but there's always room for improvement."

My head rocked back and forth as I listened to him speak. I could tell he had a little hustle in him, but he seemed like he would fold if shit got too hot for him. "Spoken like a potential go-getter. So, you the muscle man, huh?"

"I done knocked out a few niggas that got in the way. I ain't no professional when it comes to dealing or no shit like that, but I'm willing to learn the game." Kamari was very confident and fluent with his answers.

"Experience can be a brutal teacher. You sure you ready for that?" Off the strength of Skeet, I wanted to give him a shot, but I was still on the fence about him. There was definitely going to be a test to see if he would be an asset or liability. I didn't have the time or energy to deal with a snitch.

"I was born ready. All I need is a shot to prove that to you." Kamari looked me in my eyes and said that statement with pure conviction.

"What you think, bruh?" Coop was my number two, so I glanced at him for his approval.

"Let's give the little nigga a shot. If he fail, then we all walk away peacefully. If he passes, then we bring him on board. We need foot soldiers and if he really about that life, then we good to go."

"I'm with that." Kamari smiled when I agreed.

The ride wasn't gone be easy for the young dude and he definitely had to prove himself if he wanted to rock with the Brick Money Boys. Skeet got on because Coop vouched for him and he turned out to be solid. I got up and pulled a Ziploc bag from my back pocket and slid it across the table.

"That's an ounce. Come back when you get rid of it."

Kamari caught the bag as it slid in his direction. Then, he picked it up and held it in the air. "I got you, man. I'll be back soon."

"That remains to be seen. There's no timeframe, so I'll just see you when the product is sold."

Now that I made my point, I sat back down with my elbows resting on the chair and hands folded. "The meeting's adjourned." Skeet and Kamari got up and pushed in their chairs, but I stopped my protégé. "Skeet, be back by nine. We have work to do tonight, and don't be late."

Skeet stopped all movement. "We can just stay. I have nothing else to do."

"This is a private business matter and he's not a part of the team just yet. Go handle ya' business and come back."

"Okay. Cool."

Coop waited until they were gone and swiveled his chair in my direction. "Why you gave that muthafucka a ounce? What if he don't come back wit' it? Then, I'm gone have to run down on his ass."

"Nah. If he bucks, then Skeet paying for it." There was some shit I wasn't worried about and Kamari's situation was one of them. "And, if I bring him on and he fuck up, Skeet gone be responsible for taking the nigga out."

Coop nodded his head. "That's a tough decision, boy."

"Hell, yeah. Remember, back in the day, we went through the same shit. We had no choice but to make it work, 'cause we wasn't killing each other."

"Yeah man. We came a long way."

"What you say?" I agreed with a slight chuckle. "All we wanted to do was sell dope, buy jewelry, kicks and cars."

Coop laughed as we reminisced about our road to riches. "And fuck ho's. Don't forget that part."

"Shiidd. That was number one. Them young whores saw what we was rocking and dropped the panties quick. We didn't even have to tell them our real names."

"Whoo! Hoo! Them was the days and then Danielle came along." Coop's cellphone rang and his whole demeanor changed, just like that. "Speak of the devil."

"Sis know just when to call you, I swear."

"Watch this bullshit." He answered the phone and put it on speaker. "What's up, wifey?"

"Wifey my ass, when you coming home?" She yelled so loud, I thought she was standing behind us.

Coop was doing his best to keep his composure. "After I finish working, damn. You need to calm yo' ass down, 'cause you starting to piss me off."

"Well, it's better to be pissed off, than pissed on," Danielle snapped.

"Whatever, man. I'll deal with you when I get there."

"Colton Jackson." Danielle only called him by his government when she was mad.

"Stop calling me that shit."

"That's your name." Danielle exhaled hard into the phone. "Let me tell you something. I didn't get married to feel alone or for the title. I did it because I love you, but if you force my hand, I will leave you. And then you won't have to worry about tending to the needs of your wife."

"No, you listen. Love don't pay the bills and money don't cheat, so you figure it out."

Coop hung up the phone and placed it face down on the table. His eyes looked tired and I could tell he was tired of fussing with her. My ace shook his head and frowned. "You still thinking about getting married?"

"That's a damn good question," I replied.

Chapter 20

Daman

Zuri had me hotter than the summer heat in Florida. After all the shit we went through, she called it quits and left me with no remorse. Instead of losing one child, I now lost two. Losing my daughter's love hurt me more than Legend's death. In this game, there was only two ways out and that was death or jail. It's what came with the territory. I had plans for me and Zuri when I got out and she just ruined them. That shit crushed my soul to find out she was letting some nigga raw her and get her pregnant.

The past few days were hard for me and I didn't know if I was coming or going in my cell. Majority of my time was spent looking at pictures of her on my phone and in my mail stash. I missed yard calls and all. The warden relieved me of my duties for a while, so I could mourn my son's death properly. Several times I was tempted to call her, but I had to respect her wishes in order to keep up with her. I couldn't afford to lose all contact with her. The love I had for her went beyond words and no one would ever understand the way I felt or how it all started.

Zena, the love of my life, walked away from me for good after bearing all three of my kids. Legend was the oldest, so he understood what was going on. Zuri, on the other hand, was too young to make any sense of it and Mehzani was only a baby. I could admit that I wasn't the easiest to deal with, but at the end of the day, I loved my family and I would do anything for them. There were times that I got a little too drunk or hit a line or two and became physical.

My means of income was hustling and I was great at it. So great, I easily became the number two to my distributor. He liked the way I worked and manipulated every situation he was faced with. One day, he approached me, saying he needed me to go out of the country to meet up with a new supplier. I was up for the task since he was paying a pretty penny to travel.

The only thing I was worried about were my kids and their safety while I was away. To put my mind at ease, he sent my family to live at one of his safe houses where they would be protected and kept under surveillance at all times by his brother. Fast forward one month later, I finally came back to the states and Zena was upset because of the amount of time it took. Little did she know, that trip paid me five hundred thousand dollars and that meant we were moving into our very own house.

Eight months later, she gave birth to a mixed child and I knew there was no way on earth that baby could be mine. After a while, she finally admitted to sleeping with my distributor's brother and announced she was moving out. To say I wasn't hurt would be a lie, because I wanted to kill her and that baby. The only thing that saved her were my kids. I knew if I ended up in prison no one would take care of my kids the way I did. Needless to say, I made her leave without telling my kids goodbye. In my eyes any woman willing to leave her children wasn't worthy of being a mother.

"Daman, please let me tell my kids goodbye and that I love them," Zena begged.

"No. You don't love my kids, so get the fuck off my porch with that mutt you call a son. You will never see them again," I spat.

After tossing out all of her things in the middle of the night, I went back inside the house and came up with an explanation as to why they would never see their mother again.

Fast forward two years later, Zena made zero attempts to see our kids. I was fine with it, but it was affecting Zuri badly. One night, I was sitting on the sofa watching a movie, when I received the phone call that would destroy me forever.

"Hello."

"Is this Daman Monroe?"

"Who the fuck is this?"

"This is Detective Santos from the Gainesville Police Department. I'm calling about Zena Haynes."

"What about her? I haven't seen Zena or heard from her in years."

"How do you know her?" he probed.

"She was the mother of my children before she abandoned them years ago." I turned off the television and sat up in my seat. The tone of his voice had me worried.

"Well, I'm sorry to tell you this over the phone, but last week we found remains of a female victim inside a cement tank. Apparently, she had been in there for a while. We received a positive match from her dental records."

My heart shattered into a billion pieces and my hands shook uncontrollably as I forced myself to keep the phone to my ear. "What do you mean, remains?"

"Zena had gone missing just about two years ago. Her boyfriend reported her to authorities after she didn't return from a store run. Now, he was a person of interest, but he had a solid alibi and there was no physical evidence, so we were forced to release him."

My mind was running wild and then it all made sense as to why she never bothered to call or visit them. There was no doubt in my mind, he killed her for the simple fact that he had a wife. I cried for Zena because I couldn't protect her, and I cried for Zuri because she would never see her mother again in life.

"I'm so sorry for your loss, sir. If we make any arrests, I'll be sure to contact you. Her family has been notified and they will be here sometime tomorrow, if that helps."

"Thank you."

After I hung up the phone, I went into the kitchen and found the strongest bottle of liquor I could find. I was in luck, because I had a gallon of gin. For the next few hours, I got drunk and high. The amount of lines I snorted that night was extremely high and I ultimately lost count. Zena's death had really taken a toll on me and I felt somewhat responsible for her demise. I pushed her away into the arms of another man chasing the dollar and, in the end, he killed her.

My emotions were all over the place and I found myself crying off and on. I was set on destroying myself because I wasn't over her and she still had my heart. There were some women in my life, but they didn't last long because Zuri often ran them off. In between my mourning I dozed off for a little while and when I opened my eyes, Zena was standing in front of me smiling.

"What the fuck?" I mumbled. It had to be a dream, because she was dead. The detective had just confirmed that.

It was crazy because she looked so youthful and as beautiful as I remembered. Zuri was definitely her twin. Zena walked up to me and touched my face. It made me shudder, but it felt good because I missed her terribly. Her reasons for leaving me no longer mattered and I wanted to hold her, so I pulled her close to me. Our lips connected, but it was like she forgot how to kiss me. That didn't matter, because I took the lead. I needed to show her how much I missed her.

She was wearing a nightgown, so I raised it and rubbed the spot between her legs where all three of my seeds entered the world. It was warm down there and I was anxious to taste her. I laid her down on the couch and licked her pussy slowly, but she didn't moan. In fact, she was quiet the entire time I ate her out. My dick was hard and I wanted to feel her. I removed my pajama pants and boxers, then climbed on top of her. My head was throbbing, as I rubbed it against her lips to get her moist. Thrusting my hips forward, I tried to ease my way in, but she was too tight. Back to the drawing board, I licked and slurped on her pearl until she was wet. Once more, I tried to push myself in, but she screamed out in pain.

"Daddy, that hurts."

The sound of her voice scared me and I jumped up. That was when I realized it was Zuri.

The knock on my cell door brought me back from my past. "It's open," I shouted.

The door became ajar and in walked Tate. She had a serious look on her face, but I wasn't worried about anything she was about to say.

"Williams," she called my celly's name. "Can you give me and Monroe a moment?"

"Sure thing." He climbed from the top bunk and landed on his feet. "How long?"

"It'll be brief, so you don't have to go too far," she replied. "Just watch the door for me." Williams nodded his head and walked out the door, making sure he closed it behind him.

"How are you?" Tate stepped close to my bunk and glanced down at me.

"I'm maintaining." I was lying on my back, still in deep thought.

"I was worried about you. I texted the phone, but I didn't get a response."

Tate knew about my son's murder, since she was the one that helped me get shit through these walls for my business. "Yeah, I know. I wasn't in the mood to talk. Still processing that shit."

"I understand." She bent down and grabbed my dick. "I miss you in the laundry room."

"Yeah, I know." That's all she was worried about in the first place. It was funny how much power the dick had.

"Can I get a sample? We short-staffed tonight, so we don't have anything to worry about and Williams watching the door."

At that point, words weren't needed because she seemed to have a solid plan in place for us already. I had a little built-up pressure, so I was down for the cause. I freed my limp dick from my gym shorts and she got straight to it. There was no sense in wasting time. We both knew why she made her presence known. Closing my eyes, I ran my fingers through her hair weave while she concentrated on rocking the mic.

Tate tried to suck the skin off my dick. I guess she really missed me in the laundry room real bad. She had me gritting my teeth and wiggling my toes. The slurping noises were music to my ears. As bad as I wanted her to keep going, I had to stop her before I busted a nut in her mouth. On a sly tip, I eased my hand by her lips and pulled it from her mouth.

"Let me up." Tate licked her lips all seductively and shit, then wiped the remnants of the pre-cum from the corner of her mouth. Loosening her belt and pants, she stepped over to the sink and let them fall to her ankles. There was plenty of privacy because I always kept paper over the small window on the door, but I wasn't dropping my pants though. Bending my knees, I positioned myself behind her and pushed my way inside her wet pussy. She definitely came ready.

First, I started out slow, but then I sped up a bit. It had been so long and her shit felt much tighter that day. She must've taken a vinegar bath or some shit to tighten that thang up for me. Her lips gripped down on my shaft hard, suctioning it like it was giving me head too.

"Yeah. Yeah," We moaned together like we had been waiting for this very moment for months.

"Ooh. Ss."

Using my left hand, I wrapped it around her throat. "Shh."

The deeper I dug in them guts, the more she tried to throw it back, but no one needed to hear all that voluptuous ass clapping. So, I squeezed down her neck some more.

"Be still. I got this."

"Yeah," she whispered, tossing her head to the side and biting down on her lip in pleasure. "Mm. This is just what I needed."

Instead of responding, I closed my eyes and kept grinding. My only focus was catching a nut, so I could take a nap when I was finished.

"Arghh." That shit was coming and fast too. "Be still. I'm coming," I warned. The end was near, so I thrusted harder and harder. "Fuck. Fuck."

"Ooh, daddy, catch that nut."

My eyes shot open and my dick deflated when she spoke those words. All I could think about was Zuri and the way she called me that shit. Now, she was out there calling another nigga daddy, fucking and sucking him with no condom. Tate really fucked my nut up. I snatched my dick out with an attitude and pulled up my pants. This shit had to stop and it needed to stop at that very moment. No nigga had any business fucking my daughter. God made her for me and my job as a father was to love and protect her at all times. That nigga couldn't love her the way I did, and he couldn't do the shit I did for her. The solution was simple, he had to go. Once he was out of the picture, she would come back to me and we would be together again.

"Why you stop?" Tate snapped.

"I got mine," I lied. Hell, it wasn't like she knew if I did or didn't.

"No and you know I didn't."

"Oh well, I'm tired. I'm about to hit the shower." I smacked her on the ass and gathered my shit for the shower. Tate was hot, while she fixed her clothes aggressively. After she put herself back together, she stormed out without another word. I didn't give a fuck though. Shit, I was trying to save my baby girl and I knew just who to call for help.

***

Rock

"Hello."

"What's up, brother?"

"Nothing much, brother. What's going on with you?" Daman didn't sound like himself and I knew Legend's death played a major role. Then on top of that, the situation we were currently dealing with.

"What you doing?" he asked.

"Sitting in the Popeye's parking lot."

"Remember that business we discussed? The surveillance job I said I may need soon."

"Yeah."

"Well, it's time to get rid of it, and I mean like yesterday. The subject is bad for business and standing in the way."

"I'm in the area, so I'll handle it as soon as I leave here." I was on Sunrise Boulevard, so I was about ten minutes from her house.

"Okay. Hit me when it's done."

"I'm on it. Talk to you later."

"Rock," Daman called out.

"What's up?"

"Don't let nothing happen to my daughter." Daman's voice was filled with concern, but he had nothing to worry about. Zuri wouldn't be around when I took him out.

"Zuri will be safe. Trust me."

"Okay."

After I finished the rest of my chicken, I cleaned my hands, tossed the box out the window and drove off. Daman and I had been friends for many years and there was nothing I wouldn't do for him and vice versa. When I first learned about his relationship with his daughter I was in utter disbelief, but I never judged him for it. When you come from a background of polygamy and Mormonism, you tend to look away from certain things. My family was big on those things, but that wasn't something I believed in, so my mom allowed me to choose my path and moved us away. To each his own was my thought process and as long as he wasn't forcing her, I stayed out of their affairs.

The streets were dark and the neighborhood was quiet. Daman definitely picked a good spot for his daughter to be safe in. I parked my truck across the street the same way I always did, but this time I was backed in at the empty house that was for sale. Zuri's car was in the driveway and so was the guy's car, who I presumed to be her boyfriend. The lights were on inside the house, so I got comfortable. My shotgun was on the backseat and my Ruger was in my lap.

Daman didn't go into detail about why he wanted the boyfriend dead, but ten grand was enough to make me not give a fuck. If he wanted me to lay him out, then that's what was about to happen as soon as I saw him.

For the next hour, I was a sitting duck. Since I started the stake-out, he rarely drove his car and mainly rode with the dude I saw him with. The chicken box I consumed was kicking in and I suddenly had a case of the drops. My eyes were heavy as shit, but I couldn't afford to go to sleep. Opening up my console, I pulled out a pack of cigarettes to have a smoke.

Somewhere between twelve and one, I fell asleep because when I opened my eyes, all of the lights were out in the house. That meant one of two things, I missed him coming in or he was already in there and they had gone to bed. It was okay because I had a solution to that as well. Before I prepared to get out the truck, I opened my glovebox and took out a small tracking device. The coast was clear, so I got out the truck and crept across the street. Quickly, I stuck the device underneath the car. Operation Brick was in full affect. When I turned around, I could see someone standing on the porch looking in my direction, so I walked off casually as if I was strolling the block.

Chapter 21

Brick

"Oh, my God, you trying to kill me," Zuri moaned tirelessly, while pushing her hand against my rock-hard abs to keep me from sinking deep.

"Nah. I'm trying to knock out every thought you may have in your head about having a one-night stand."

"I'm not even thinking about that." Zuri's eyes rolled to the back of her head when my body outweighed the strength in her hands, allowing my dick to hit the bottom. "Ow. Shit."

"Better not."

Zuri's legs were stretched wide open in the bed like the letter V. One leg was on my shoulder, while my body straddled the other, delivering the best dick she ever received in life. Deep long strokes was on the menu, after eating the pussy for an appetizer. The way I was balls deep in that ass, I felt like I had been deprived of the cat for weeks. When in fact, it had only been a few days. She held back sex after I made her quit her job, so now she had to reap the consequences of her actions.

Insecure was nowhere in my vocabulary, so I wasn't worried that she would fuck somebody else. I knew better. I was just talking shit. As I slow grinded against her pelvis in a circular motion, I hit every inch and corner her walls had to offer.

"Ooh. Ah. That hurt." Zuri bit down on my arm like she was trying to break my skin, but I wasn't fazed. It actually felt good.

"You should be used to it by now."

Putting her hands in the way wasn't going to make me stop period, let alone biting me, so all of her attempts were useless. The noises she made only stroked my ego. Besides, she was so cute and sexy when she whimpered and bit her lip when I put it down. Those fuck faces were everything to me. Leaning forward, I slipped my tongue into her mouth with some slight aggression. That was the only thing that would muffle the noises, not that it mattered to me.

She could holler until the neighbors came knocking and I wouldn't care.

Passionate sex was good and all, but I liked that rough shit. There was just something about it that drove me insane. Slowly caressing her breasts, my hand made its way up to her neck and I squeezed it, but not too hard. That made me a little more aggressive and my strokes that much faster. The thrust of my hips was fast with short strokes, and I was doing to my best to keep from pounding the life out the box. I would hate to fuck up the baby because the snatch was too good.

Back and forth I slid rapidly, knocking the juice out the box. My dick glistened as I watched it disappear over and over. The warmth of it made me want to stay in it all day, but she had to catch a flight in the next two hours. Pregnant pussy would have any man sprung and I could vouch for that. The sensation from me rubbing her clit fast increased the speed of her breathing, and I knew she would be coming shortly. Nice guys finished last and I wanted to make my baby come first.

After a while, my dick started to throb against her vagina walls. That heavenly feeling was finally near. "Shit. I'm cumming," I grunted, while biting down on my lip.

"Good." Zuri was lucky it was too late to stop my orgasm, because I would've folded her slick talking, raspy voice ass up for another twenty minutes.

***

One hour later, we were pulling up at the airport and as promised, Mehzani was standing at arrivals. Zuri looked at me, but her expression was very hard to read.

"Are you okay?" I asked.

"Yeah. I'm okay. It's just been so long since I've seen my sister." The emotion in her voice was thick as smoke. I've missed her so much."

"I know and that's why I did it. Your relationship with your sister is important and I would love to see y'all create a bond." I parallel parked the car and put it in gear.

"I know and that was very sweet and thoughtful of you." Zuri's eyes were becoming glassy. "Thank you."

"You're welcome and you don't have a reason to cry, so dry your eyes and go have fun. You deserve it and as long as I have breath in my body, you will continue to see days like this. I promise you that."

She nodded her head and grabbed her purse. "Okay."

I grabbed her chin and tilted her head in my direction. "Come here." Zuri leaned towards the driver's seat. "I love you."

"I love you too," she replied, then I kissed her passionately.

We both opened our car doors and I jogged over to the passenger side to help her get out. Mehzani came closer to the car. "Is everything okay?" she asked out of curiosity.

"Yeah, she's okay. Just a little emotional behind everything. How are you?"

Mehzani shook her head up and down smiling hard. "I'm so excited. I've never been to Cali."

"Me either." Zuri walked over and hugged her sister tightly with so much compassion. "This is going to be so much fun." While they were having their moment, I pulled her rolling suitcase and carry-on bag from the backseat and placed it the sidewalk.

"I know, right?" Mehzani screeched.

"Be careful and call me the second y'all land." I reminded both of them.

"I will."

"Enjoy spending my money," I teased.

"Don't you worry, we will, bruh." Mehzani caught me off guard with that, but I was cool with it. It was important for me to build a relationship with her sister as well, so I gave her a hug.

"Keep an eye on my babies."

"I will," Mehzani replied with a lot of confidence that she would make good on her promise and I believed her.

After releasing my hold of baby sis, Zuri stepped up and kissed me once more before they walked off. "Be safe, baby."

***

A few hours later, I found myself pulling up at Coop's place. He was sitting in the parking lot waiting on me.

"Whaddup, bruh?" He dapped me up. For some reason he had this big-ass grin on his face.

"Fuck you grinning for?" I folded my arms across my chest and leaned against his car.

"Danielle been blowing my shit up all fuckin' night. I told her the shit was dead, but she ain't trying to hear none of that shit."

This nigga had the craziest wife in Florida and he had the nerve to stay out all night. "Sis 'bouta kill yo' ass and I don't want no parts of that shit."

"Nah, bruh. Come in with me." He grabbed my arm. "What the hell happened to you?"

"Hell, nah. Don't put me in that shit and Zuri bit me," I answered every question in one wind, while pulling away from him.

"Too late, bruh. I told her that we fell asleep at the house after we finished splitting up the product." Coop looked down at his phone. "See, her ass calling again."

"Y'all muthafuckas' crazy. Damn. Bring ya' ass on." Coop knew how to fuck up a wet dream. The last thing I needed was Danielle thinking I had him out all night.

"I love you, bruh." He patted me on the back.

I swatted his hand. "Fuck outta here with that shit. Where the fuck you was at anyway?"

Coop looked at his phone screen before he responded. "I went by this chick house and fucked around and fell asleep over there."

"And you wonder why she always flipping out on your ass. You be warranting that shit. Trying to make it seem like she crazy."

"Chill, bruh, 'cause I ain't even hit the chick. We was just Netflix and chillin'."

"You could've did that with your wife, since she wanted to do dinner and a movie. Come on and let's get this shit over with."

"Why the hell she bit you?" Coop was really interested in my affairs.

"Damn, you still on that?"

"Hell, yeah."

"I was delivering the goods and shit got a little too deep, so to speak." The expression on his face was worth a million words just by the way his mouth dropped to the floor. His eyes were big and buggy and I couldn't do shit but laugh. That's what he got for being so goddamn nosey.

With Zuri gone, I planned on spending the majority of my time working and spending quality time with Breanna. Coop stood at the front door of his condo and took a few deep breaths. That shit was funny as fuck.

"Don't get scared now. Open the door, nigga." I pushed him into the door and he hit it with a hard thud. "That was in case you wanted to change your mind and leave."

"And you say I play all the time." Coop unlocked the door and we walked in.

Danielle was cooking when we walked in the house. "Well, look what the cat dragged in." She rolled her eyes and sipped her wine.

"Yeah, I brought your husband home." Technically, I did.

"You could've left him at the bitch house he was at." She was ready to snap, like she spent all night preparing what she was gone say.

"What I told you, bruh? She wasn't gone believe me." Coop walked up and tried to kiss her.

"Move. I don't know where your mouth been."

"Man, I was with this nigga," Coop tried explaining that lie once again.

"Colton, get the fuck away from me with that lie before I toss this boiling water on your ass. You expect me to believe that two grown-ass men, with women, chose to sleep in a traphouse instead of going home?"

"Sis, chill. It's true. That shit wasn't intentional, 'cause I had to take my lady to the airport this morning." This nigga had me hard-down lying to his wife. Thank God Danielle and Zuri wasn't friends, because he would've been shit out of luck.

"I bet she cussed you out too." Danielle looked at me for clarification.

"No, she didn't because as a woman, she knows her place," Co-op yelled like a crazed maniac and sat down on his recliner, while I sat on the sofa. The two of them were a match made in hell when shit was bad, but when it was good, they had a great relationship.

"Shut up, fool," Danielle spat. "I'm not talking to the cheater."

"My lady understands what I have going on and she don't give me a hard time. She knows I'm not doing any cheating and besides, I sent her to California for a few days, so she good."

"Well, that's good for her. I don't trust your brother, 'cause he full of shit." Danielle pulled a pitcher from the fridge. "You want something to drink?"

"Yeah. What's that?" The pitcher was dark, so I couldn't see the contents.

"Grape Kool-Aid."

"Yeah, let me get a cup."

"Bae, can I get a cup too?" Coop loved to be facetious and that's why Danielle stayed on his ass.

"Sure. Give me a second," she replied sweetly. That damn girl had a split personality above all else.

Danielle hit the corner with a smile on her face and handed both of us a glass. She then kissed Coop on the forehead. "I'm sorry, baby. I believe you."

"It's cool, wifey." Coop raised the glass to his lips and took a big ass gulp. Seconds later, he spit all of it out onto the carpet and gasped desperately for air. "What the fuck you put in that glass?"

"Fabuloso, you lying-ass bastard. Did you think I would forgive you that easily? You just wait, because you will reap what you sow and I promise you that."

Danielle stormed off in the direction of their bedroom. All I could do was shake my head and holler. "Nigga, she got yo' ass good."

Coop jumped up and ran into the kitchen. I could hear him opening and closing the cabinets. "This muthafucka done lost the little bit of marbles she did have." He held the bottle of Fabuloso in the air, so I could see it. "She gone make me fuck her up."

A few minutes later, Danielle scrolled from the back with her bag on her shoulder. "Have a good day Brick." She smiled.

"Coop. Get out here and fix this shit man." I stood up and rushed towards the kitchen.

"Her ass ain't going nowhere." That's what his lips were saying, but her actions showed otherwise. Danielle opened the door and slammed it behind her.

"Bruh, go stop your wife."

Coop and I ran out the door in pursuit of her, but she must've run down the stairs or some shit. By the time we made it to the parking lot, she was tossing her bag into the car and climbing inside. He ran up to the driver's side and grabbed the door. I stood there and watched to see if a fight was gone break out before I intervened.

"Danielle, don't do this. I'm not mad about you trying to poison me, so let's go back in the house and talk about this."

"You think I give a fuck because you not mad? No. I don't care and that's why I did it."

Time was flying like a muthafucka, because Zuri was calling my phone already. I answered her call. "Hey, baby. You just landed?"

"Yes."

"How was your flight?"

"It was nice, thanks to my baby getting us first-class seats." That happiness in her voice made my heart melt. All I wanted to do was make her and my daughter happy.

"That's good."

"What you doing? And what is all that noise?"

"Over here in the parking lot at Coop house, listening to him and his wife argue."

Zuri laughed. "Oh, well, good luck with that."

"I know right, but I'm…" The shouting was elevating by the second and Coop's voice caught my attention.

"Get down, bruh."

The sound of panic in his voice caused my head to swivel in the opposite direction. I saw Coop running towards me at a fast pace. At first, I was confused, but then I finally caught sight of what he was looking at. It was the barrel of a shotgun. My heart rate sped up, being that I was unprepared for what was happening. In slow motion, my phone slipped from my fingertips and hit the concrete. The next thing I heard were multiple gunshots that clapped like thunder.

To Be Continued…
Corrupted by a Gangsta 3
Coming Soon

Submission Guideline.

Submit the first three chapters of your completed manuscript to ldpsubmissions@gmail.com, subject line: Your book's title. The manuscript must be in a .doc file and sent as an attachment. Document should be in Times New Roman, double spaced and in size 12 font. Also, provide your synopsis and full contact information. If sending multiple submissions, they must each be in a separate email.

Have a story but no way to send it electronically? You can still submit to LDP/Ca$h Presents. Send in the first three chapters, written or typed, of your completed manuscript to:

LDP: Submissions Dept
Po Box 870494
Mesquite, Tx 75187

DO NOT send original manuscript. Must be a duplicate.

Provide your synopsis and a cover letter containing your full contact information.

Thanks for considering LDP and Ca$h Presents.

Destiny Skai

Coming Soon from Lock Down Publications/Ca$h Presents

BOW DOWN TO MY GANGSTA

By **Ca$h**

TORN BETWEEN TWO

By **Coffee**

BLOOD STAINS OF A SHOTTA **III**

By **Jamaica**

WHEN THE STREETS CLAP BACK **III**

By **Jibril Williams**

STEADY MOBBIN

By **Marcellus Allen**

BLOOD OF A BOSS **V**

By **Askari**

LOYAL TO THE GAME **IV**

By **T.J. & Jelissa**

A DOPEBOY'S PRAYER **II**

By **Eddie "Wolf" Lee**

IF LOVING YOU IS WRONG... **III**

LOVE ME EVEN WHEN IT HURTS

By **Jelissa**

TRUE SAVAGE **V**

By **Chris Green**

TRAPHOUSE KING **III**

By **Hood Rich**

BLAST FOR ME **III**

By **Ghost**

ADDICTIED TO THE DRAMA **III**

By **Jamila Mathis**

LIPSTICK KILLAH **III**

CRIME OF PASSION

By **Mimi**

WHAT BAD BITCHES DO **III**

THE BOSS MAN'S DAUGHTERS **V**

By **Aryanna**

THE COST OF LOYALTY **II**

By **Kweli**

SHE FELL IN LOVE WITH A REAL ONE **II**

By **Tamara Butler**

LOVE SHOULDN'T HURT **II**

By **Meesha**

CORRUPTED BY A GANGSTA **III**

By **Destiny Skai**

A GANGSTER'S CODE II

By **J-Blunt**

KING OF NEW YORK

By **T.J. Edwards**

CUM FOR ME **IV**

By **Ca$h & Company**

<u>**Available Now**</u>

<u>RESTRAINING ORDER **I & II**</u>

By **CA$H & Coffee**

<u>LOVE KNOWS NO BOUNDARIES **I II & III**</u>

By **Coffee**

<u>RAISED AS A GOON I, II, III & IV</u>

<u>BRED BY THE SLUMS I, II, III</u>

BLAST FOR ME I & II

By **Ghost**

LAY IT DOWN **I & II**

LAST OF A DYING BREED

BLOOD STAINS OF A SHOTTA I & II

By **Jamaica**

LOYAL TO THE GAME

LOYAL TO THE GAME II

LOYAL TO THE GAME III

By **TJ & Jelissa**

BLOODY COMMAS I & II

SKI MASK CARTEL I II & III

By **T.J. Edwards**

IF LOVING HIM IS WRONG…I & II

By **Jelissa**

WHEN THE STREETS CLAP BACK I & II

By **Jibril Williams**

A DISTINGUISHED THUG STOLE MY HEART I II & III

LOVE SHOULDN'T HURT

By **Meesha**

A GANGSTER'S CODE

By J-Blunt

PUSH IT TO THE LIMIT

By **Bre' Hayes**

BLOOD OF A BOSS **I, II, III & IV**

By **Askari**

THE STREETS BLEED MURDER **I, II & III**

THE HEART OF A GANGSTA I II& III

By **Jerry Jackson**

CUM FOR ME

CUM FOR ME 2

CUM FOR ME 3

An **LDP Erotica Collaboration**

BRIDE OF A HUSTLA **I II & II**

THE FETTI GIRLS **I, II& III**

CORRUPTED BY A GANGSTA

By **Destiny Skai**

WHEN A GOOD GIRL GOES BAD

By **Adrienne**

A GANGSTER'S REVENGE **I II III & IV**

THE BOSS MAN'S DAUGHTERS

THE BOSS MAN'S DAUGHTERS II

THE BOSSMAN'S DAUGHTERS III

THE BOSSMAN'S DAUGHTERS IV

A SAVAGE LOVE **I & II**

BAE BELONGS TO ME

A HUSTLER'S DECEIT I, II

WHAT BAD BITCHES DO I, II

By **Aryanna**

A KINGPIN'S AMBITON

A KINGPIN'S AMBITION **II**

I MURDER FOR THE DOUGH

By **Ambitious**

TRUE SAVAGE

TRUE SAVAGE II

TRUE SAVAGE **III**

TRUE SAVAGE **IV**

By **Chris Green**

Destiny Skai

A DOPEBOY'S PRAYER

By **Eddie "Wolf" Lee**

THE KING CARTEL **I, II & III**

By **Frank Gresham**

THESE NIGGAS AIN'T LOYAL **I, II & III**

By **Nikki Tee**

GANGSTA SHYT **I II &III**

By **CATO**

THE ULTIMATE BETRAYAL

By **Phoenix**

BOSS'N UP **I , II & III**

By **Royal Nicole**

I LOVE YOU TO DEATH

By Destiny J

I RIDE FOR MY HITTA

I STILL RIDE FOR MY HITTA

By **Misty Holt**

LOVE & CHASIN' PAPER

By **Qay Crockett**

TO DIE IN VAIN

By **ASAD**

BROOKLYN HUSTLAZ

By **Boogsy Morina**

BROOKLYN ON LOCK I & II

By **Sonovia**

GANGSTA CITY

By **Teddy Duke**

A DRUG KING AND HIS DIAMOND I & II

A DOPEMAN'S RICHES

Corrupted by a Gangsta 2

By Nicole Goosby

TRAPHOUSE KING I & II

By **Hood Rich**

LIPSTICK KILLAH **I, II**

By **Mimi**

BOOKS BY LDP'S CEO, CA$H

TRUST IN NO MAN

TRUST IN NO MAN 2

TRUST IN NO MAN 3

BONDED BY BLOOD

SHORTY GOT A THUG

THUGS CRY

THUGS CRY 2

THUGS CRY 3

TRUST NO BITCH

TRUST NO BITCH 2

TRUST NO BITCH 3

TIL MY CASKET DROPS

RESTRAINING ORDER

RESTRAINING ORDER 2

IN LOVE WITH A CONVICT

Coming Soon

BONDED BY BLOOD 2

BOW DOWN TO MY GANGSTA